THE CASE OF THE
VANISHING
CORPSE

400

THE CASE OF THE
VANISHING CORPSE

KEL RICHARDS

Hodder & Stoughton
An imprint of Hodder Headline Australia

For Shane and Sarah

A Hodder & Stoughton Book

First published in 1990 by
Hodder & Stoughton (Australia) Pty Limited
Reprinted 1991

Reprinted in 1994 by
Hodder Headline Australia Pty Limited,
(A member of the Hodder Headline Group)
10-16 South Street, Rydalmere NSW 2116

National Library of Australia Cataloguing-in-Publication data

Richards, Kel, 1946- .
    The case of the vanishing corpse.

    ISBN 0 340 53601 2.

    I. Title.

A823.3

Typeset in Australia by G.T. Setters Pty Limited
Printed in Australia by Griffin Paperbacks, Adelaide
Cover illustration by Mike Worrall

Author's Note

Just as Shakespeare performed in modern dress is still Shakespeare, so history in modern dress is still history. Despite the telephones, guns, cars and pizzas that you will find in this book, the central events of the story are real historical events. In other words, *The Case of the Vanishing Corpse* is history in modern dress. (A note on the source documents will be found at the end of the book.)

Chapter 1

'I've brought you a thermos full of nice hot chicken soup.'

'Mama, you shouldn't have.'

'It'll do you good.'

'But Mama, it's embarrassing.'

'So now you're embarrassed by your own mother?'

'It's not you I'm embarrassed by, Mama, it's the chicken soup.'

'So now I'm not allowed to make my boy some chicken soup.'

'I'm thirty-seven years old!'

'To me you're still my baby. If you'd married some nice girl it'd be different. Why you and Rachel never—'

'Mama, please stop going on about me and Rachel. It just never worked out, that's all. And stop bringing me chicken soup.'

'Enough already. I can't stay here to be insulted by my own son, I've left the gelfilte fish on the stove. I'll just do a quick dust, and I'll leave.'

'Just *leave*. The office doesn't need dusting.'

'What you really need is a good secretary. Rachel still hasn't found a job—'

'Mama!'

'All right! All right! I'm going. I'll see you at dinner.'

As she left she couldn't help giving the glass panel in the middle of my office door a quick wipe over. It didn't need it. You could read the lettering quite clearly:

Ben Bartholomew
Private Investigator
Missing Persons A Specialty
(No Divorce Work)

Alone in my office again I could sit and think. Not that I had much to think about. Business was very quiet. A few weeks ago I'd had more cases than I could handle and I'd had to pass some work on to my old friend Sam Solomons. But that was during Passover. During Passover there are always lots of people here in Jerusalem, and lots of work for me. There's always someone who's gone missing or some jewellery that's been snatched. But, as I say, that was a few weeks ago, and now the whole place was as quiet as a tomb.

Inactivity is something I just can't stand. Sitting around waiting for the phone to ring is not my idea of a wonderful afternoon. So I decided to lock up the office and go cry on the shoulder of my favourite bartender, Nick the Greek. (Why does every Greek who owns a bar call it *The Olympic*? I've never figured that out. They're supposed to be creative these Greeks, but it's always *The Olympic*!)

My office is upstairs above a narrow alley that runs off the street of the coppersmiths. I got as far as the alley when I remembered the answering machine. I went back, switched the phone over to the machine and retraced my steps. When I turned out of the alley into the street all the coppersmiths were sitting under their shop awnings beating away with their little hammers, but what caught my attention was the car. A very impressive stretch limo—black, with tinted windows. What was it doing in an out of the way place like Coppersmith Street? Waiting for someone? Yes— for *me*!

As I walked past, the limo's back door flew open, a hand the size of a camel's foot reached out, grabbed me by the shoulder and dragged me into the back seat.

'Hey! What's the idea—'

'Shut up. The Big Man wants to see you.'

The Big Man? Why would Big Joe Caiaphas want to see me? He was the centre of all the action in Jerusalem. Whatever was going on in town he knew about, and got ten per cent of it. Even his legit front was big time—high priest at the temple and chief liaison with the Occupying Government. This was his town. What would he want with a small time Private Eye?

I was about to find out.

The limo pulled up behind the back wall of the temple. The guy with the big fists and deep voice bundled me out of the car and in through a low, wooden doorway. Obviously, I was not making an official visit.

'Follow me,' he rumbled.

I followed as meek as a sheep. He led me through winding staircases and down narrow corridors dimly lit by just the occasional small, high window. I stumbled once in the dark, and my guide snapped, 'Hurry up! He's waiting.'

At last we came to a large, dark, polished timber

door. My guide knocked three times, opened it and pushed me inside. The door closed behind me.

I was in a very big, very dim room. It took me a while to make out that down at the end of the room was a large desk, and behind the desk—shrouded in darkness—was a figure. And it was the Big Man himself.

When he spoke it was barely above a whisper. 'Thank you for accepting my invitation, Mr Bartholomew. Take a seat. Make yourself comfortable.'

There were some large, soft cushions scattered around the room. I lowered myself onto one, but I was careful not to relax.

'I have a job that needs to be done, Mr Bartholomew.'

'Well, I'm a bit busy at the moment,' I lied, 'but I'd be happy to put my other cases to one side.'

'I was sure that you would. This job is of the utmost urgency, but it must be handled with the greatest discretion.'

'Oh...sure, sure. Discretion—that's my middle name.'

'In placing this case in your hands, Mr Bartholomew, I am depending on your discretion, and on your...peculiar skills. Should you fail me in this matter I'm afraid that my Mr Shagmar will have to pay you a visit—a visit that neither of you would very much enjoy.'

'Mr Shagmar?'

'My special assistant. He escorted you here today.'

'Oh...that Mr Shagmar.' I swallowed hard. 'Well, what's the job?'

'You have a reputation, Mr Bartholomew, for finding missing persons.'

'Yeah, I'm good at that.'

'Good. There is a missing person I want you to find. But this will be a little different to most of your cases, Mr Bartholomew, since the man I want you to find is not only missing—he is also dead.'

'Dead? You sure?'

'Positive. I pronounced the death sentence myself.'

'Dead, eh? Well, that shouldn't be too hard. I know every cemetery in Jerusalem, I'll start there.'

'If it were as simple as that, Mr Bartholomew, I would not be calling on your special services.'

'I guess so. What's the story then?'

'On the Friday of Passover week we arranged with our colleagues in the Occupying Government for the execution of three criminals.'

'Yeah, I remember. Two thieves and that political guy.'

'Correct. And, it's that "political guy", as you call him, who is giving us trouble.'

'He's dead but he won't lie down, something like that?'

'Something like that, indeed. Were you in Jerusalem during those executions?'

'No, I was up in Jericho. Tracking down the runaway teenage daughter of this rich merchant guy who—'

'Since you weren't here I will explain. The political agitator and blasphemer Jesus Davidson died quickly, before sunset in fact.'

'Lucky for him. I've seen guys hang on there for days.'

'Quite so. As soon as he died his friends took his body, and, before the sun set and the sabbath began, they buried him in a borrowed tomb.'

'Can you tell me where?'

'Mr Shagmar will give you the details. Because this Jesus Davidson person had a dedicated group of followers, mostly wild, unpredictable Galileans, I considered it wise to place an armed guard over the tomb.'

'Sensible precaution.'

'In a manner which I have not yet got to the bottom of, at some time over the next thirty-six hours my guards were overpowered and the body stolen.'

'Sounds like the work of fanatics to me.'

'One assumes so. At any rate, this man's followers are now going around claiming that their leader is not dead, but has, in fact, conquered death.'

'Come back to life? Ridiculous!'

'Exactly. Intelligent people like you and I can see that, Mr Bartholomew, but the world is full of simple, gullible people all too ready to believe such blasphemous nonsense.'

'Well—it should be pretty easy to put a stop to it. Just produce the body.'

'If we could, we would. I want you to find it for me, Mr Bartholomew. That is your task. Bring me the body of Jesus the Nazarene!'

Chapter 2

And that was all he had to say. With a swirl of his robes he swept out of the room. I stood up, feeling a little shaky. This was not going to be easy. On one side political and religious fanatics, on the other side the Syndicate, and in the middle—me.

The door opened. Shagmar, the ungentle giant, was there. 'I'll take you back to your office, Bartholomew,' was all he said, then he led the way through the maze of stairwells and passages to the back door and the big limo.

As we drove back to Coppersmith Street, with the driver honking his way through all the peddlers and donkeys, Shagmar handed me a piece of paper.

'Here's the address of the tomb,' he said. 'This is the last place the body was seen.'

I looked at the address on the paper. It was a garden tomb on the city boundary.

'Who was on guard when the body disappeared?' I asked.

Shagmar snatched the paper back and scribbled a

name on the back. 'That's the man,' he said. 'He's had some sort of nervous breakdown, and he's on sick leave at the moment. I've written my telephone number underneath. As soon as you get a strong lead, call me.'

'Will do.'

'And here's a photograph of the missing man. It'll help you identify the corpse.'

'Sure thing. Tell me, Shagmar, do you really believe his followers stole the body?'

'Who else would want to take it?'

'I guess you're right. But this is a city of intrigue and I was wondering. . .'

'What?'

'What about the OG? Could they have taken it?'

'Why would the Occupying Government want to do a thing like that? But you should check it out. Check every possibility. And there's another thing. . .'

'Oh, yeah?'

'I haven't told the Boss—I didn't want to worry him—but it did occur to me that since Davidson died, or appeared to die, so quickly, maybe he didn't die.'

'Just fainted you mean? And then revived in the coolness of the tomb?'

'It's a possibility. And if he's really on his feet and walking around somewhere that means trouble—big trouble. So you'd better check that out too.'

'Will do. Now there's just one other thing—the little matter of my fee.'

Shagmar grabbed my collar and pulled me towards him. With our faces only two inches apart he hissed at me, 'Understand this, little man. For this case we are paying you the biggest fee you will ever get—your life!'

And with that he flung me into the corner of the limo's plush back seat. I sat up and pulled my coat straight.

'Well, I'm glad we've got that sorted out,' I said.

A few minutes later I was bundled out of the car, and found myself standing in the late afternoon sunshine, back where I had started, in Coppersmith Street. My first thought was for Nick the Greek. More than ever I needed that drink.

The Olympic was cool and shaded on that hot afternoon. It was almost deserted. There was a drunk in the corner, a tart waiting listlessly for a customer, and Nick himself behind the bar.

'Your best brandy—and make it a double,' I said as I hoisted myself onto a bar stool.

'This is the real stuff,' said Nick. 'Genuine Egyptian. And what's wrong with you? You look like you've seen a ghost.'

'It's not a ghost I've seen, Nick, it's a ghost I'm looking for.'

'Uh? That don't make no sense.'

'This afternoon, Nick, ol' buddy, nothing makes any sense.'

'What's the matter, Ben? Tell your Uncle Nick all about it.'

I took a long, deep drink of my brandy, and then I started. 'Jesus Davidson, Nick, you remember him?'

'Sure. I even saw him once. At the start of Passover week—there was a big procession.'

'Right, that's the guy.'

'And by the end of that week his number had come up. The system had caught up with him. It was a case of here come the soldiers, and bye-bye Jesus.'

'That's half the story.'

'Half? What's the rest of it?'

'The execution didn't take. Three days later he's back in business again.'

'Are you kidding me, or what?'

'I'm just telling you, Nick, what's being said around town.'

'Really? That's the buzz, is it? Amazing stuff, man.'

Just then the tart sidled up to me.

'Beat it, sister,' I said. 'I'm not buying what you're selling.'

'And you think you know what I'm selling?'

'Yes. Some exotic form of venereal disease picked up from the grottiest Roman soldiers in the whole empire.'

'Well, that's where you're wrong, mister. What I have to sell you is information.'

'What sort of information?'

'I can give you a line on the Jesus crowd. That's what you want, isn't it?'

'So you heard, did you?'

'I couldn't help hearing. And I know you're a Private Eye so I guess you want to get a line on these people.'

'What would someone like you know about that lot?'

'I'm not telling—I'm selling.'

I pulled out a ten dollar bill and waved it under her nose. 'Only if the information is worth it.'

She eyed the bill hungrily. 'My old room-mate,' she said, 'she joined them. I've got a forwarding address.'

'What's your ex-room-mate's name?'

'Mary. . . Mary Magdalene.'

'Okay, sister, you've got a deal.' I picked up a coaster off the bar and gave it to her. She wrote down an address on the back, then we swapped the coaster for the ten spot. The bar was starting to fill up, so I took my drink to a corner table and looked at the address on the back of the coaster. It was on the other side of town, near the markets. A shadow fell across the table. I looked up. It was the drunk who had been sitting in the corner of the bar.

'I heard what you were talking about,' he slurred. 'And I've got something to tell you.'

I thought he probably just wanted a free drink, but I learned a long time ago that at the start of a case you never knock back any possible source of information. So I waved him to a seat, and signalled Nick to bring another couple of drinks.

The drunk attacked his drink like a camel hitting an oasis.

'I'll buy you another one,' I said, 'if you've got some useful information.'

'Jesus Davidson you were talking about?'

'That's right.'

'I ran into him once. He ruined my life.'

'Oh yeah?'

'Yeah. I used to have a good job. I was a beggar.'

'You couldn't be a beggar. There's nothing wrong with you. You've got to be a cripple to be a beggar.'

'I know, I know. I used to be a leper.'

'Listen, buddy, no one used to be a leper. Once you're a leper, you're always a leper.'

'Yeah, yeah, that's what I thought. When I first got leprosy I thought my life had ended. My family cast me out. No one wanted anything to do with me.' He took a drink, he seemed to find his memories painful. 'I became a beggar, of course. It was the only thing I could do. And I fell in with some others. We used to work the main roads and the big towns as a group. There were ten of us. Lepers do all right. People throw money at you to keep you away.'

Then he started to sniffle. 'Oh no,' I thought, 'a crying drunk.'

He wiped his eyes with the back of his hand and said, 'I got used to it. You can get used to anything, I guess. Then Jesus Davidson came by—and he healed us. The others, the nine who used to beg with me, they got jobs, they learned trades. I just couldn't cope with being normal again. I can't seem to hold a job, or make any friends. The others are doing okay, but not me.'

'You weren't listening the first time, buddy. Leprosy is incurable.'

'Look. Look, I'll show you.'

He dug into his coat and pulled out two grubby pieces of paper and pushed one of them across the table at me.

It was a certification of Leprous Uncleanness signed by one of the temple doctors. Then he showed me the second piece of paper. It certified him to be Completely and Ritually Clean.

'These two papers can't belong to the same person,' I said.

'They're mine, all right. They're both mine,' he sniffled.

As I got up and left him, he was crying into his beer again. It was starting to hit me that this was going to be one weird case.

Chapter 3

By the time I stepped out of Nick's bar, the sun was hanging low in the western sky. I decided to take a look at the scene of the crime before it got dark. I hailed a passing cab and told him to take me to the Fish Gate.

'Hey, buddy,' said the driver, 'you know why they call it the Fish Gate?'

'Why?'

'Because it stinks.'

'You just drive. I'll make the jokes.'

We'd hit the peak hour, so the drive was slow. The streets were filled with tired office workers and shop assistants hurrying home. At last the cab crawled to my destination. I paid off the driver and got out. He was right about the stink. 'The Council should do something about it,' I thought as I made my way to the gate in the city wall called the Fish Gate.

I walked through the huge, arched gateway, and found myself standing on a rocky slope. I pulled out the piece of paper Shagmar had given me and checked the address. A few minutes brisk walking brought me to the garden where the tomb was located. The garden gate was open. I walked a few paces inside. An old man carrying a pitchfork stepped out from behind a tree.

'Two bucks,' he said.

'What's that?'

'If you want to see the empty tomb, it'll cost you two bucks.'

'Who are you?'

'I'm the gardener. Two bucks if you want to see the tomb.'

'Look, I have official authorisation to inspect the tomb.'

'Show me. Show me your authority.'

'Okay. . .' I reached inside my coat and whipped my thirty-eight calibre, snub-nosed revolver out of the shoulder holster it always nestled in.

'How does that look for authority?' I asked.

'That's official enough for me,' he said. 'You can't blame a guy for trying to make a buck.'

'Have there been many people wanting to see the tomb?'

'Not huge crowds, but groups. You know, three or four. Sometimes half a dozen. So I thought to myself, what the heck, I'll make a few bucks out of it.'

'And have you?'

'Have I what?'

'Made a few bucks?'

'Yeah, I got a little for my retirement fund.'

'Now show me the tomb.'

'It's this way. Follow me.' He led me down a flagged path between flower beds and rows of bushes.

As we walked I asked him, 'Were you here when the body disappeared?'

'Not me. I was at my sister's place in Bethany. Big feast times, like Passover, they're family times, you know. And since my wife died fifteen years back I always go to my sister's place at Bethany for Passover. I don't get on too well with her husband, but it's still like family, you know. . . Here it is.'

The garden ended abruptly in a rocky cliff face. The tomb was an oblong that had been cut directly into the rock face, like an artificial cave.

'It must have taken a while to cut that tomb straight into the rock.'

'Months. It took them months.'

'And who does it belong to?'

'Joseph Arimathea. Rich guy. Member of the Council.'

'I've heard of him.'

I made a mental note to call and see him. If I could get past his secretary, that is. He had a reputation for being a hard man to see.

Leaning up against the cliff face, beside the open tomb, was a large circular slab of stone. This would be the stone 'door' that would be rolled across the entrance of the tomb to seal it.

'That stone'd take a bit of moving,' I said.

'Takes two men—if you're not in a hurry.'

'And if you are in a hurry?'

'If you're in a real hurry, you forget about it. It just doesn't move quick, that stone.'

'Yeah, I see.'

'Makes a racket too.'

'What does?'

'Moving the stone. Makes enough noise to wake the dead.' Then he grinned. 'Bad choice of words.'

'Mind if I look inside?'

'You're the man with the gun. Do what you like.'

I stepped in. There was not much room. On one side a shelf had been cut into the rock. That's where the body was laid to rest. Then I got a shock, a real shock.

'Hey, Pop! Who's been fiddling with things in here?'

'No one, son, that's exactly the way the tomb was found. No one's been allowed to touch anything.'

I backed out of the narrow tomb and turned to face him. 'In that case, there's something I don't understand.'

'I know. Everyone notices the same thing—the graveclothes.'

'That's right. The winding sheet, the shroud, everything's still on the shelf in there. Undisturbed.'

'As if the body just sort of dissolved and melted right through them. That's right, son, that's what everyone says who looks in there.'

'How do you explain it, Pop?'

'Me? I can't explain anything. But it makes it worth two bucks, doesn't it?'

I was as confused as a camel in Cairo. It just didn't make any sense: a huge, stone slab that took two men to move, and graveclothes that were undisturbed. Whoever had stolen this particular corpse were the weirdest bunch of grave-robbers I'd ever come across.

As I turned and walked out of the garden I threw the old man two silver dollars. 'Here you are, Pop,' I said. 'For your retirement fund. You were right—it was worth two bucks.'

By the time I got back to the city gate dusk had turned into darkness, and the streetlights had come on. I had to walk several blocks before I came to a cruising cab. I gave the driver the address that the tart from *The Olympic* bar had written on the back of the coaster.

24

I sat in the back of the cab watching the yellow streetlights pass, and feeling the hum of the city around me.

I got the driver to drop me off at the markets.

The stalls were all closed and shuttered, but the cafes and bars were open and the neon signs were twinkling. The night was warm and the sidewalk tables were inviting. I decided to have a coffee and get my bearings. So I flopped into the nearest cafe chair. It had been a long day and I could feel a headache coming on.

'Coffee,' I said to a hovering waiter, 'with lots of cream.'

When the coffee arrived I added a little brandy from my hip flask and a generous helping of sugar to give me energy. The coffee was sensational, I could feel it doing me good.

The waiter was still hovering. (It was a quiet night.)

'Hey, buddy!' I called. 'You got a minute?'

'Yes, sir.'

'Do you know where this address is?' I showed him the coaster.

'Yes, sir. It's a fair distance from here, I'm afraid, sir. Four, maybe five blocks. Actually it's closer to the temple than the markets.'

I asked him for specific directions, paid for my coffee, tipped him, and left.

Half an hour later I was standing in front of the building that, according to the tart in Nick's bar, was Mary Magdalene's new address. It was a plain, two-storey house. The sort of house you'll find all over Jerusalem. It had been whitewashed in the last six months.

I knocked on the door. The knocks echoed inside. There was no other sound, and the house didn't show a light. I knocked again. There was no response and no sound from inside. I gave the door a good, solid pounding. Still nothing.

'You're wasting your time.' The voice came from a little fat guy who had appeared in the front doorway of the house next door. 'There's no one there.'

'I'd figured that out.'

'They've all gone away.'

'Do you know where?'

'Who are you looking for?' he asked, ignoring my question.

'Mary Magdalene.'

'Forget it. She's gone straight. She don't take customers no more.'

'But she does live here?'

'Oh sure. Or, at least, she did. With the others. But they've gone away, like I said. I don't know if they're coming back.'

'Who are the others? Who did she live with?'

'Oh, a whole crowd of people. A religious mob. It was sort of a commune. Personally, I'm glad they're gone. They used to make an awful racket. Every night they'd have a sing-song. And when they weren't singing they were chattering away. Always talking and laughing and joking.'

I began to think I must have come to the wrong place. 'Is this crowd who I think they are—the Jesus Davidson mob?'

He nodded.

'Why would they be laughing and singing? Their leader was executed three weeks ago.'

'Yeah, I know. I got two, maybe three days of peace when that happened. Then all the noise and singing started up again.'

'That doesn't make any sense.'

'They're religious—nothing makes any sense.'

'I still need to find them. Do you know where they've gone?'

'How could I not know? They talk so loud. There's a big, redheaded fisherman who sort of runs the show these days. He's got such a voice. He could call Cairo without a phone that guy.'

'So where is it? Where have they gone?'

'Galilee.'

'Galilee is a big place. Where in Galilee?'

'How should I know? All I heard them talk about was Galilee.'

'They didn't mention the hills or the lake?'

'Not that I heard.'

'They didn't mention Capernaum? Bethsaida? Nazareth?'

'Nope.'

'Well, look... If they come back, or if you remember anything else, give me a call.' I handed him one of my business cards. 'I'll make it worth your while.'

He held the card close to his eyes and squinted at it. ' "Ben Bartholomew",' he read. 'Hey, I read your name in the newspaper once. When they ran that series about runaway kids. You found a lot of them for their parents, didn't you?'

'Yeah, that's me. So, if anything turns up, give me a call. Okay?'

'Okay.'

The night was mild and balmy, so I decided to walk home. The back way took me through twisting, dark alleyways and narrow streets. I was breaking one of my own rules: when you're on a big case don't walk down dark alleys—specially at night. About halfway home I was forcibly reminded of the rule.

I was just passing a shadowy doorway when someone came at me from behind. A leather-gloved hand smothered my mouth and a large knife was pressed against my throat.

Chapter 4

Someone else grabbed my arms and propelled me into
the back of a car. I wondered for a moment if I was
being summoned to Big Joe Caiaphas again. But this
was no stretch limo, it was a beat-up old Fiat. That's
what's wrong with being part of the Roman Empire—
too many Fiats.

As the car started up I was blindfolded, a gag was
stuffed into my mouth, and my hands were tied
behind my back. So, if it wasn't Caiaphas who was
having me picked up, who was it? Judging from the
car, some cheap hood. Even though I was blindfolded
I could tell from the turns the car was making that
we were leaving the temple area and heading towards
the southern end of the city. That confirmed it—
one of the smaller gangs had picked me up. I knew
where they'd be taking me, too—Cheesemakers
Valley it was called. Only there weren't any
cheesemakers there any more. The name was
centuries old. Nowadays the place was home for all
the cheap hoods in Jerusalem.

The driver pushed the car along fast, the tyres squealing around corners. When, with a screech of brakes, we came to halt, I was pulled roughly out of the car and into a building. Still blindfolded, I was pushed along from behind, stumbling and banging into the walls of a narrow corridor as we went. I heard a door open. I was dragged inside and my blindfold was taken off.

It was a long room with a low ceiling. The only light came from a single, naked light bulb. The only furniture was a pool table, some crates of beer, and three rickety chairs. I was shoved onto one of these by the hood behind me. Leaning on the pool table and staring at me was one of the cheapest hoods in Jerusalem—Barabbas.

'Leave his gag in, and his hands tied up,' he said. 'He doesn't need to say anything—just listen.'

So, that's who had grabbed me: the Barabbas gang, a mob of small-time smugglers and stand-over men.

'Did you hear what I said, punk—I want you to listen.'

When I didn't respond I got a sharp fist in my kidneys from the hood behind me.

'Are you listening now, punk?' asked Barabbas.

I nodded.

'Good. Little Ben is learning his lessons. Now here's the lesson I want you to learn, punk. You've been stirring up the mud, and I want you to stop.'

I must have looked puzzled.

'Jesus Davidson! That's what I'm talking about,' explained Barabbas, impatiently. 'Did you know I was supposed to be executed that day? Well I was. It was my day. My time was up. But it was Passover, so the governor offered to release one of the prisoners. We figured that might happen, so my boys were all there and they yelled out my name real loud, and I got the nod.'

He walked around the room in silence for a minute, then sat on the edge of the pool table. 'That was a smart move on the part of my boys. Yeah, a smart move.' He got up again and walked towards me. 'And the result was that Jesus Davidson kicked the bucket instead of me. Well, better him than me any day.'

He leaned over me, breathing beer and garlic in my face. 'But I don't want to be reminded of it, see. I'm supposed to be a tough guy. Having someone else wiped out instead of me is bad for my reputation. So I want it forgotten.'

He walked across to one of the crates of beer, took out a can, and ripped the top off. 'Forgotten,' he said, wiping his mouth with the back of his hand. 'People forget about these things. A nine day wonder, that's all it is—' He took another swig of beer. '—as long as some little punk doesn't go around reminding them—stirring things up.'

I had a feeling it was Barabbas who was having trouble forgetting. He hadn't shaved, and his eyes were bloodshot.

'I don't know who your client is, punk.'

I wished he'd taken the gag out of my mouth for just a minute. He would die of fright if I told him my client was the Big Man himself, the man who allowed the little gangs like his to operate, and who raked off ten per cent of their profits.

'I don't know who your client is, punk, and I don't care. Just drop it, that's all. Unless you want both your legs broken in seventeen places you'll stop snooping around. Yeah, I know the corpse is missing. I don't know who took it, and I don't care. I just want you to stop stirring the mud.'

He walked back over to where I was sitting. 'You got the message, punk? Has little Ben understood his lesson? Here's something to make sure you don't forget.' With surprising speed he leapt forward and buried his fist in my stomach.

As I gasped for air, my blindfold was put back on, and I was dragged back to the car. Once again we squealed and screeched through the back alleys of the city. While I lay on the back seat, getting my breath back, the hood sitting beside me untied my hands.

At one corner the old Fiat slowed down, slightly, the back door was opened and I was flung out onto the road. I must have hit my head on the gutter as I fell, because I felt a sharp pain, and then tumbled into a well of inky blackness.

When I had come to, pulled the gag out of my mouth and untied the blindfold, my watch showed a little after eleven o'clock. I pushed myself to my feet, somewhat unsteadily, tucked my shirt back into my trousers, and staggered home.

I let myself in through the front door but I hadn't taken three steps inside the hall before—

'Benjamin, is that you?'

'You were expecting someone else? It's too late for the paper boy and too early for the milkman. Yes, Mama, it's me.'

Then she walked into the hall, threw up her hands and let out a sort of choked scream.

'*Eeeeee!* What's happened to you?'

'I fell over, Mama, that's all.'

'You expect me to believe that? Fall, schmall. Tell your Mama what really happened.'

'It doesn't matter, Mama. I fell. That's good enough.'

'It's not good enough for me. Do you think I like to see

my boy looking like this? Do you think it warms a mother's heart that her boy comes home beaten up?'

'Just don't worry, Mama,' I said as I turned and walked into the sitting room.

My papa was there, sitting in his favourite armchair, in his dressing gown, reading the evening paper.

'Evening, Papa.'

'Evening, Benjamin.' Papa raised his eyes from his evening paper and looked me up and down. 'Hard day at the office?'

'You could put it like that.'

I poured myself a stiff drink. 'You like one of these, Papa?'

'A small port would be nice.'

I poured him his drink, and threw my tired body into an armchair as Mama came back into the room.

'I'm heating up your dinner for you,' she said.

'I'm not sure I'm hungry.'

'You've got to eat to keep up your strength. And you've got to get yourself out of this dreadful profession you're in.' With that she turned on her heels and left the room.

A couple of stiff drinks, one of Mama's big dinners, and a hot shower repaired the day's damage. The next morning I felt as good as new.

At nine o'clock I bounded up the narrow stairs full of energy, and let myself into my office.

It wasn't empty.

For a start, my files were scattered all over the floor. And for seconds, there were two men waiting for me—big men, wearing dark glasses and leather jackets. One was sitting in my chair behind the desk. The other was leaning against a filing cabinet.

It was the one behind the desk who spoke. 'Good morning, Mr Bartholomew', he said. 'Take a seat.'

Chapter 5

I looked at the two guys who were filling my office with a miasma of menace. Neither of them was pointing a gun at me, but the threat was unmistakable. I sat down.

As I did so the man behind my desk flashed a badge at me. I recognised it at once: RIA—The Roman Intelligence Agency. There are some people who say the expression 'Roman Intelligence' is an oxymoron (look it up in your Funk & Wagnalls). On the other hand you've got to admit that the Romans are an inventive people. Just look at all the things they've invented: roads, Fiats, dry cleaning fluid. Mind you, the only reason they invented dry cleaning fluid was because they'd invented spaghetti first, and they had to get the Bolognese off their togas.

The RIA are not guys you mess around with. These babies have so much authority from the emperor himself they can break any law they fancy. If they mark your file 'Terminate With Extreme Prejudice' then you might as well make your will—there's no escape. So, the last thing I wanted was to make a couple of RIA guys unhappy.

'How can I help you, fellahs?' I asked.

'We have a grapevine,' said the one behind my desk, 'a very effective grapevine.'

'I believe you.'

'And we have heard, Ben—you don't mind if I call you Ben, do you?'

'No, no. I'd like you to be friendly, real friendly.'

'That's nice, Ben. As I was saying, we have heard that you've got yourself involved in a political case. That right, Ben?'

'Well...sort of political, I guess.'

'Tell me about it, Ben. We had a quick check through your files, but we couldn't find anything.'

'I haven't written up my case notes yet.'

'In that case, I guess you'll just have to tell us about it.'

The guy leaning on the filing cabinet wasn't saying a word, he was leaving it all to Mr Charming behind my desk.

'Well, it's about the political agitator, Jesus Davidson,' I said. 'He was executed on the Friday of Passover week, and now his corpse has disappeared. I've been hired to find the corpse.'

'Is that all you've been hired to do, Ben?'

'That's all. Honest.'

'And who's your client, Ben?'

'That's confidential. I mean, I'm supposed to maintain the confidentiality of my clients. You understand that, don't you?'

'Of course we do. Now, tell us the name of your client, Ben.'

'Aw, come off it, fellahs.'

'Would you like to come back to the Fortress

Antonia with us? We can find a nice, quiet, soundproof room for you to talk to us in.'

I could hear the rattle of chains and torture equipment in his voice. I thought about his proposition for exactly seven seconds. 'All right, all right. Big Joe Caiaphas...that's who hired me.'

The two RIA men threw puzzled glances at each other.

'You want me to believe your client is Caiaphas, Ben?'

'That's right. Would I lie to you?'

'No, Ben, I don't think you would. But why does Big Joe want the body found?'

'He says he's worried about the Davidson mob. Instead of dispersing and bringing the whole movement to an end, they're still around and going as strong as ever.'

'Our grapevine tells us the same thing.'

'Apparently they are claiming that he didn't die. Or rather, that he did die, did really die, and then came back, victorious over death.'

'Yes, we've heard the same story, Ben. In fact, we know that when Jesus Davidson was being buried your client came to His Excellency, the Governor, and asked for permission to put a guard over the tomb in order to prevent the followers from stealing the corpse and making exactly this sort of claim. But, despite that, they appear to have done it.'

'Looks like it.'

'And it's the political ramifications that worry us, Ben. His Excellency has had trouble in the past with hysterical nationalism and he doesn't want any more in the future. You understand?'

'I understand all right.'

'So, we'd like to be kept informed about the progress

of your investigation. You have no problems with that, do you, Ben?'

'Oh, none at all, none at all. I'll let you know if I come up with anything.'

Then the guy behind my desk pushed back the chair and stood up. 'You've been very co-operative, Ben,' he said. 'We like that. Here's my card. Call me if you find anything.'

He handed me his business card, and they both left. His companion had still not uttered a word.

It was a plain, white card with a telephone number printed in the middle. No name, no anything—just a phone number.

I stuck the card in my wallet, and, with a sigh, began cleaning up the mess. After wasting ten minutes trying to sort out the files that had been thrown all over the floor, I decided this was a dumb game and I didn't want to play any more. I pulled a cardboard box into the middle of the room, shovelled all the papers into it, and pushed it into the far corner of the office, out of sight. One of these days, I told myself, I'd be able to afford a secretary and she could sort all those old files out again.

Back at my desk I switched on the electric jug. The day had not started well and I needed a mug of strong coffee. While I was sipping it I called my friend Sam.

'Solomons' Investigations, can I help you?' It was a young female voice.

'Ben Bartholomew calling, may I speak to Sam?'

'Hold the line, please, and I'll see if Mr Solomons is available.'

There was a pause and a click and then Sam came on the line. 'Morning, BB. How are you doing?'

'I'm doing fine. Since when could you afford a secretary, Sam?'

'I can't. She's my kid sister—she's on work experience.'

'I should've guessed. Listen, Sam, I need a couple of favours.'

'Well, I guess I owe you one.'

'You owe me a couple, Sam.'

'Don't push it, BB. What do you want?'

'First of all, do you still have your contact at the barracks?'

'Yeah, we keep in touch.'

'Can you speak to him for me? I want to find out who was on duty at the executions on the Friday of Passover week.'

'That's easy. I'll buy him a drink at lunchtime. I'll have the information for you by tonight.'

'And there's one other thing. Can I borrow your four-wheel drive for a few days?'

'The old Landrover? Ever since that trip down to Sinai it's a real rattletrap, you know?'

'Yeah, I know. Can I borrow it?'

'When do you want it?'

'Maybe tomorrow, maybe the day after. As soon as I've finished checking out a few leads.'

'How far do you want to take it?'

'To Galilee. I'll be away a couple of days.'

'Okay, okay. As long as you pay for the petrol you can borrow it.'

'You're a good man, Sam.'

'Mind you, I'm not sure it'll make it all the way to Galilee and back. But if you're crazy enough to try it in my old Landrover, good luck to you.'

'Thanks, Sam.'

'Now you owe me one, BB. I'll call you tonight.'

After I'd hung up, I pulled a foolscap pad out of my desk and began writing up my case notes. In point form I listed all the facts I had gathered so far in my interviews with witnesses. I filled several pages, slipped them into a manila folder marked 'Davidson', and dropped it into the top drawer of my desk. Just as I finished, the phone rang.

'Bartholomew's Detective Agency. Ben Bartholomew speaking.'

'Good morning, Bartholomew.' I'd recognise that throat full of gravel any time—it was Shagmar. 'Are you making any progress?'

'It's early days yet, Shagmar, don't press me.'

'I am pressing you, Bartholomew, and I intend to press you harder. This is important, and the Big Man wants an answer.'

'You tell Caiaphas to keep his pants on and give me a little time. I'll get there.'

'You'd better, Bartholomew, you'd better.'

I had a sinking feeling in the pit of my stomach that this was a case I should never have got involved with. I was already being pushed by the tough guys from the Syndicate, by the Barabbas gang, and the RIA, and I had the religious and political fanatics, suspected of stealing the corpse, still to come.

'And there's another thing I rang you for,' continued Shagmar. 'I can give you a lead you might find useful.'

'Tell me more.'

'He's one of the agents we had following the Davidson crowd around. He's staying at a farmhouse just out of town. I can give you the address. Write this down.'

I wrote it down. 'What's his name?' I asked.

'Eleazar. And you'll have to pay for any information he gives you. But don't worry—we'll cover your expenses. Get on with it, Bartholomew. You don't have time to sit around.'

'Before you go, Shagmar. There's something else you can do for me.'

'What's that?'

'Get Barabbas off my back. He had me picked up last night, and threatened me. He wants me to drop the investigation. It embarrasses him.'

'I'll get him straightened out. He won't bother you again.'

'Thanks. And there's one other thing you should know—I had the RIA drop in on me this morning.'

There was a long silence on the other end of the phone.

'Did you hear me?'

'Yeah, I heard you. What did they want?'

'A progress report on this vanishing corpse case.'

'*Hhhmmm.* Well—don't let it worry you. You just get on with your job, Bartholomew.'

And with that, he slammed down the phone.

Chapter 6

I locked up my office and left a few minutes later. To get to the farmhouse where this Eleazar character was staying I'd have to leave the city through the Valley Gate. That was some distance from my office, but it was a warm, sunny morning and I decided to walk.

I had walked no more than two blocks when I recognised someone on the other side of the street.

It was Rachel.

My heart did flip-flops and the adrenalin started to pump. I had just never got over that girl. For a full minute I was in an agony of indecision: should I try to speak to her, or should I just pretend I hadn't seen her?

Then she spotted me. She smiled and waved. And that was all the encouragement I needed. I ran across the crowded road, dodging around the donkeys and camels, to where she stood.

'Hi!' I said.

'Hi. How are you keeping?'

'Oh, well. Real well.'

'I'm pleased to hear that.'

'And yourself?'

'I'm just fine.'

'You're looking terrific—as always. Look, have you got a few minutes? How about a cup of coffee? There's a cafe just over there.'

'Okay. I'm waiting for some friends, but I'm about ten minutes early. Let's have some coffee.'

Rachel was nine years younger than me, but she always seemed very mature and sophisticated—even when I first met her, around five or six years ago. And right now I was in a cold sweat like a seventeen-year-old on his first date, and she looked as calm and controlled as ever.

She ordered a flat white and I ordered a Vienna, then I sat and looked at her. Her hair was black, and her eyes were a warm, dark brown. Her face was more angelic than ever.

'You haven't changed,' I said.

'Oh yes I have. We're all changing, all the time.'

'Does that mean that you've become...?' I left the question dangling.

'Less religious? Not in the least,' said Rachel, picking up my dangling question and dropping it with a clunk on the floor.

'Rachel, we were so close. We had so much in common. We went to the same concerts, we liked the same restaurants, we laughed at the same jokes... And then you came all over religious.'

'I still like the same concerts, and restaurants and jokes, Ben. It's just that there's an extra dimension in my life now.'

'The trouble is your whole life revolves around the new dimension. And I'm just not a religious sort of guy.'

'You believe in God, don't you?'

'Yes, of course I believe in God. But I've got to get on with living my life.'

'The truth is, Ben, that you *are* religious. Everyone is, if only they realised it. Whatever it is that beats at the heart of your life, that is your religion. Whatever your life is centred on is your "religion". Do you understand what I'm trying to say?'

'I understand, all right. So, what's my real religion then?'

'I guess I'd say that you really enjoy your work. Even when it gets rough you enjoy it. And when you're not working, you still pursue enjoyment. Whether it's reading a book or getting drunk, you're pursuing enjoyment. I'd say, enjoyment is your religion. It's the central organising principle of your life, so that's your religion.'

'So what's wrong with that? What's wrong with enjoyment?'

'What's wrong, Ben, is that I used to have the same religion as you. When you took me out to hear John the Baptist three years ago—'

'Worst mistake I ever made.'

'—I realised that I'd put something else where God should be in my life. If God is really there, then you can't treat him like some second cousin from Cairo. You've got to treat God like God. For the past three years I've been working through the business of making God the centre of my life.'

'And in the process, I lost you.'

'We drifted apart, Ben. I didn't suddenly "get religious". I changed my religion—from the pursuit of enjoyment to the pursuit of God. Our hearts were no longer on the same things. Our priorities were different, and . . . Watch what you're doing with that sugar.'

I looked down at my cup. I suddenly realised that

43

I had been shovelling sugar into it without keeping count. 'How many spoonfuls did I put in?' I asked sheepishly.

'Four. . .I think,' said Rachel with a grin.

'Maybe if I don't stir it, it'll be all right.'

For a mintue or two we drank our coffee in silence. Finally, I found the courage to say, 'I miss you, Rachel.'

She looked down at her coffee cup. 'I miss you too,' she said quietly.

After that there didn't seem to be much else we could say. The sun was still shining, and the air was still and warm, but I shivered a little.

'What case are you on?' asked Rachel, I think mainly to break the silence.

'The Jesus Davidson case,' I said.

Her eyes lit up. 'Really? What about the case?'

'Apparently his corpse has vanished.'

'So, it's true then,' she said softly, more to herself than me.

'And I've been hired to find it'. Then I was struck by a suspicion. 'You haven't become one of this Jesus crowd, have you, Rachel?'

'No,' she said. 'At least, not yet. But I know some of the women in that group. They're really sweet. And I was devastated when he was killed. It was a tragedy. He was the greatest Jew of our generation, Ben, you've got to believe that.'

'I don't know much about him.'

'Actually, I'm waiting for two of the women from the group now, Susanna and Joanna. I'm meeting them this morning.'

'I thought they'd all gone up to Galilee.'

'Most of them have. But Joanna's husband is a steward in Herod's court, and they've been held up in Jerusalem on official business.'

'Listen, since you know them, maybe you could introduce me and. . .'

'No, Ben! Don't make use of me for your job.'

'No, you're right. I don't want to do that,' I reached across the table and laid my hand gently on hers. Rachel took my hand and gently squeezed it as she looked into my eyes and smiled one of those wonderful, warm smiles of hers.

'Oh, Rachel, you're still the most magic woman I've ever known—'

'Good grief! There they are. I can't keep them waiting. I'll have to run, Ben.' My big romantic speech was interrupted.

We both stood up. As I threw some money on the table to cover the bill, Rachel caught me completely by surprise. She stepped up to me and kissed me, full on the lips, one of those soft, warm kisses we had shared so often in the past. Then she was gone. From the other side of the street, after greeting her two friends, she turned and waved to me. Then I lost sight of her.

Chapter 7

When I reached the Valley Gate the mid-morning sun was blazing brightly. On top of which, I still had the warm, inner glow from Rachel's kiss. I took off my jacket and hung it over my arm. Before me lay the Valley of Hinnom, and on the rising slope on the other side was my destination, the farm of Eleazar.

The road was unsealed, but a city council water truck had been spraying the roadway to keep the dust down. As the water dried in the morning sun the dust rose in puffs, and whirls, and small clouds.

After twenty minutes of walking I stopped to wipe the sweat off my forehead, rolled up my sleeves, loosened my tie, and slogged on.

It took me three quarters of an hour to reach the address that Shagmar had given me. It turned out to be a vineyard. It was a big one and the vines looked well developed and healthy. This little farm would have cost a packet. But then, the Syndicate has a reputation for paying its agents well, so Eleazar would have been able to afford it.

The farmhouse was a square, white building not far from the road. I couldn't see any servants about, which surprised me. And the farmhouse itself had all its doors closed and its windows shuttered, which surprised me even more. The place had a deserted look about it. I had a sinking feeling that I might have walked a long way in the sun for nothing, but I tried the front door anyway.

My first knocks on the door provoked some sounds from inside, so at least someone was there. I pounded on the door a second time. From inside came the scrape of chair legs on the floor, the door was unlocked, the bolts were shot back, and the door swung open.

Standing inside was a dishevelled man with an unshaven chin and bloodshot eyes.

'Your name Eleazar?' I asked.

'What if it is?' he slurred, his breath puffing a cloud of cheap whisky over me.

'Shagmar sent me to see you.'

'Shagmar can drop dead.'

He started to close the door, but I put my foot against it and pushed hard. It shot open, and Eleazar staggered back into the room.

'This is important, old son,' I said. 'So don't be difficult.'

Eleazar collapsed into a chair. There was no fight left in him. 'All right, all right. What do you want?'

I pulled up a chair facing him, but far enough away to avoid the whisky breath.

'What I want, old son, is the body of Jesus the Nazarene.'

'You don't need me for that. What you need is a grave-robber.'

'Too late. The grave-robbers have already been

47

there. I want to know who took the body, and where it's hidden.'

That seemed to shock him. Suddenly he was halfway sober. 'The body's gone? You're sure?'

'I've seen the empty tomb.'

He thought for a moment. His eyes looked puzzled and he ran his fingers through his matted hair. 'Maybe the temple authorities took it,' he said. 'You know, to stop the tomb becoming a martyr's shrine.'

'No chance. It was the Big Man at the temple who hired me to find it.'

'Really? The body of Jesus is missing, and Big Joe Caiaphas doesn't know where it is?'

I noticed that he had difficulty saying the name "Jesus". He hesitated, and then sort of rushed over it.

'That's right.'

'I can't help you. I know nothing about it.'

'But you know the Davidson crowd, and you know their hangouts.'

'You don't need me. Go and talk to them. It's all in Shagmar's files. Caiaphas will have the address of every house they ever visited in Jerusalem. I tailed them for him. I reported every place they ever went. I reported everything Davidson ever said. That's why they used me as a witness at the trial.'

'What trial?'

' "What trial?" You kiddin' me? *The* trial. The Davidson trial. I was chief prosecution witness.'

'I was out of town at the time—so I don't know the details.'

'Yeah, well, I gave evidence of sorcery against... against him.'

'What sort of evidence?'

'Well, he claimed he could destroy the temple, didn't he? And rebuild it in three days. Three days! It took years to build that temple. So that's claiming powers of sorcery, isn't it?'

'And that's what they found him guilty of?'

'No. In the end they got him on a blasphemy charge.'

He took another long pull out of his bottle and continued. 'Anyway, that's all I know. Just what...he...said. And where they all went. And it's all in Shagmar's files anyhow.'

'They're not in Jerusalem. They've taken off for Galilee.'

'All of them?'

'Just about.'

'Now that I don't understand,' he said, looking genuinely puzzled.

'Come on, old son. Be a bit useful. I'll make it worth your while.'

'I don't want money!' he snapped.

'Then do it for free. But one way or another, I want some information.'

'What do you want to know?'

'Now that Jesus is gone, who would be the new leader?'

'No one could replace Jesus.'

'Okay, okay. But there's got to be some sort of leader—so, who would it be?'

'I don't know. Maybe John, he was always very close to...Jesus. Maybe Matthew. He used to be a tax official; he's a good organiser.'

'Someone suggested Peter.'

'No chance. Last time I saw him he was a totally defeated coward. He's all noise and no heart.'

'And if these people stole the body, where might they have hidden it?'

'You think *they* stole the body? You're mad!'

'Who else could have taken it? I'm checking up

49

on all the possibilities, but the strongest lead by far is that the Jesus crowd stole the corpse themselves.'

'That's crazy. Most of them took to the hills when he was arrested. On the weekend when he was buried there were only a couple of men and two or three women out of the whole group who were still in Jerusalem.'

'That would have been enough. If they'd taken the corpse, where would they have hidden it?'

'I still say you're crazy.'

'Did any of them own a tomb in the Jerusalem area they could have moved it to?'

'Of course not! Most of the followers are ordinary people—fishermen, farmers, tradesmen, public servants. They can't afford these expensive rock tombs.'

'One of the followers could. Joseph Arimathea could. He provided the original tomb, the one that's now empty.'

'But we didn't even know he was a supporter. He'd hung around a few of the public meetings, but no one knew he was a supporter until he went to the governor and asked for permission to take care of the body. No, what I said still stands: the followers are not rich people with empty tombs all purchased and standing by in case they need them.'

'Then where could they have taken the corpse?'

'I'm telling you! Just listen will you? If you think the followers took the corpse you're off the air. It's just all wrong. It makes no sense. Why would they do a thing like that?'

'Well, the rumour is, they're now saying that Jesus rose from the dead. To make that stick they'd have to steal the corpse.'

'They're saying *what?*' he hissed. His face had gone a deadly white.

'You heard me.'

'Risen. He is risen?'

'Well, they're not going around and saying it publicly yet. But Big Joe has his spies everywhere, and that's what they're saying amongst themselves all right. They say that after three days he walked out of his grave. That's why I've got to find the corpse, so they can never get away with making that claim in public.'

'You'll never find the corpse,' said Eleazar, with sudden certainty.

'Why not? I'm a good detective,' I said, but he was no longer listening to me.

'Risen? He is risen,' whispered Eleazar, talking to himself, not me. 'Is that what he meant when...? After three days? So, when he said "rebuild in three days" he meant...? He is risen...?' Then he snapped out of his reverie, turned to me and snarled, 'Get out! I want to be alone. I want to think about this.'

'No chance. Not yet, old son. I'm staying here until I get some answers that make sense.'

'You're leaving now,' he said, and as he spoke he pulled a gun out of his coat pocket. It was a four-five calibre, six-chamber revolver—the biggest handgun I'd ever seen. He had a mad look in his eye that made me believe he'd use it.

'All right, all right. Keep your shirt on. I'm just leaving.'

I picked up my coat, and edged my way back to the door, while not taking my eyes off the gun held in Eleazar's unsteady hand. He kept that cannon-like barrel pointed straight at my chest until I was right outside. Then he slammed the door, turned the key, and shot the bolts.

I walked a few yards away from the house, stood in the shade of a eucalyptus tree, and tried to work out what my next move should be.

Then I heard it: from inside the farmhouse came the loud, sharp crack of a gunshot. I guessed what had happened.

I ran back and pounded on the door. There was no response—just as I had expected. I tried putting my shoulder to the door, but it was too heavy. I tried the windows. I managed to kick in one of the shutters, prise open the window, and climb into the room. Eleazar was sprawled out on the floor. He had put the gun into his mouth and pulled the trigger. Most of the back of his head was missing.

This was something I thought it better not to be involved in. I took my handkerchief out of my pocket, and wiped down anything I might have left my fingerprints on, then climbed back out of the window and headed back to town.

It was getting on for midday by now, and the road was empty. So at least no one would see me leaving the farmhouse.

When I got back to the Valley Gate I was a lather of sweat. There was a public phone box just inside the gate. I rang the police and told them where they could find the body.

Chapter 8

I needed to get out of the sun, and I needed to sit down and think, so I headed for a pizzeria I knew. It was in a basement, and was always cool no matter how hot the day was.

That's one of the good things about being part of the Roman Empire. I guess the pizzas make up for the Fiats.

I ordered a deep-dish pizza with the works and a beer, and tried to catch my mental breath. I mopped the sweat off my forehead, took my tie right off and stuffed it into a pocket of my jacket. As I crumpled the tie into the pocket I found a couple of things that Shagmar had given me.

First there was the address of the guard, Magnus Cassius, who had been on duty at the tomb when the corpse vanished. I decided to call and see him next. He was billeted with a widow, Mrs Goldblum. I guessed that the Romans had chosen her to billet a soldier because she lived close to the military quarter—not far, in fact, from the Fortress Antonia.

The other item was the photograph of Jesus. I pulled it out of the pocket and took my first good look at it.

It had obviously been taken by one of Shagmar's spies mixing in with the crowd that always used to gather around Jesus. Jesus was in the centre of the photo, jammed in by people on all sides.

Now, Shagmar's agents are smart operators. When they take a picture like this the subject doesn't usually know he's being snapped. But Jesus knew. I could see that, as the picture had been taken, he had turned his head towards the camera. So there he was in the middle of the snap, staring straight at me.

The crowd around Jesus were blurred by movement, but Jesus himself stood out sharp and clear. It was not a handsome face. I mean, none of the big studios in Rome would have snapped him up to play a romantic lead. But he would have made a good character actor. It was a strong face. An interesting face. And those eyes looking right down the barrel of the lens seemed to be staring straight out of the photo at me. It was spooky. This was the face of a dead man, and he was looking at me, as though he was about to ask me a question. I gave an involuntary shudder, and put the photo away in an inside pocket of my jacket.

I pulled out my pocket notebook. Who else did I need to see? Ah yes, Joseph Arimathea.

'Hey waiter!' I called. 'Have you got a telephone in this place I can use?'

'Right this way, sir.'

I checked the number in the Jerusalem phone book, and then placed the call.

'Arimathea Industries, can I help you?' said a sweet voice on the other end.

'Mr Arimathea's office, please.'

'Hold the line, please.'

I waited a minute while the phone played an old Irving Berlin tune at me, then another voice came on the line. 'Mr Arimathea's office, can I help you?'

'Yes, I'd like to make an appointment to see Mr Arimathea.'

'May I have your name, please?'

'Bartholomew—Ben Bartholomew.'

'What is the nature of your business with Mr Arimathea?'

'Private.'

'I'm afraid that unless you tell me more than that, sir, I won't be able to make an appointment.'

'Listen, sister, I'm a private detective and my business concerns Mr Arimathea, not you. Just make the appointment.'

'If you'd like to hold the line for a moment, sir, I'll speak to Mr Arimathea and see if he is willing to see you.'

There was a click and I was back with Irving Berlin again. After a couple of minutes she was back on the line. 'Are you still there, sir?'

'I'm still here.'

'Mr Arimathea says he is very busy, and unless you are prepared to state the nature of your business he will not be able to spare the time to see you.'

'Tell him it's about the disappearance of the corpse of Jesus Davidson.'

She went away again. By now Irving Berlin had changed to George Gershwin. This time it was only thirty seconds before she was back. 'Hello, sir?'

'Yes?'

'Mr Arimathea will see you this afternoon at half past five, here in his office.'

'I'll be there.'

'Do you have the address?'

'Don't worry, I'll find it.'

I arrived back at my table just as the pizza was served. I ordered a second beer and demolished the pizza.

Later, in the men's room I washed my face, combed my hair, and brushed the dust off my jacket. I was starting to feel human again after my morning on the dusty road.

Just as the city was settling into its post-prandial lull I set off to find the guard Shagmar had put me on to. The address was in the maze of alleys that surround the temple area on two sides. Finding the district was easy, but once I was there half the streets didn't have names, and half of the houses didn't have numbers. I had to knock up a few neighbours before I found the right door. When I knocked a middle-aged woman answered.

'I'm looking for Magnus Cassius.'

'This is the place, so who's looking?'

'Ben Bartholomew, P.I. I have a few questions to put to him.'

'Not today you haven't. He has had a terrible shock. He took to his bed three weeks ago, and he's still not well enough to talk to anyone.'

'He has to talk to me. This is important.'

'His health is more important. Leave your telephone number. I'll call you when he's well enough to talk.'

'That's not good enough, Mrs Goldblum. I've been sent by the temple authorities, and if he refuses to talk it could cost him his job.'

She was a big woman and she was standing in the doorway. There was no way I could get past without roughing her up. And I have my code—I don't rough up mothers.

'Well, if he loses his job,' she said, 'I'll help find him another. I've written to his mother in Rome. I told her she should never have let her son go into the guards; he's not robust. He should have learned a trade. You'll never starve if you've got a trade.'

'What's wrong with your Magnus, Mrs Goldblum?'

'The doctor says it's nerves, but I say that's nonsense. He's had a shock that's all. All he needs is a mother's care and a lot of hot chicken soup.'

'Well, I've got to see him some time in the next day or two, so, tell him I've called, give him my card, and tell him I'll be back tomorrow.'

'Well...'

'I've got to see him, Mrs Goldblum, so you might as well make up your mind to it.'

With that I turned on my heel and walked off. Tomorrow would do, and if she got a chance to get used to the idea, I might avoid a noisy fuss.

Back in the middle of town, I saw Rachel again. Twice in one day. Fortune was smiling on me.

Rachel was on the other side of the busy square with her two friends, Susanna and Joanna. From a distance her friends looked like nice women—very middle class, but nice.

Just as I caught sight of them a bus pulled up. Not a local bus, but one of those coaches that do the long trips. Rachel got on the bus with her two friends and as it pulled out I looked at it's destination sign: GALILEE.

Now, why would Rachel be going to Galilee?

Chapter 9

It was hot, so instead of going straight back to the office I dropped into *The Olympic*.

Nick was in his usual place behind the bar. 'What'll it be, Ben?'

'A soda and lime juice with a dash of bitters.'

He raised his eyebrows in a silent question.

'I'm in the middle of something I don't understand, and I need to keep my head clear,' I explained. I didn't tell him that maybe it was the effect of seeing Rachel twice in one day, and remembering she always used to warn me against drinking too much when I was on a case.

My thoughts were interrupted by a drunken bellow from a remote corner of the bar. 'It shoulda been me!'

I turned towards the sound. At the table were two men. One, a big man with his back to me, was holding his face in his hands and his rounded shoulders were shaking with sobs. The table in front of him was piled high with empty glasses.

'It shoulda been me,' he roared again.

The other man was smaller. He was hidden by the shadows in the corner, and I couldn't make out his features.

The big man pushed himself unsteadily to his feet, and stood there swaying. 'I'm a dead man walking,' he slurred. 'That's what I am—a dead man walking.'

With a shock I recognised him—it was Barabbas. I turned back to Nick. 'What's going on?'

'Beats me. Those two have been here for two or three hours now. The little guy keeps buying Barabbas drinks.'

'Why would anyone want to keep feeding Barabbas booze?'

'Like I said, it beats me. And the more Barabbas drinks, the more upset he gets.'

'If there's one thing I hate, it's a crying drunk.'

'Me too.'

As Barabbas slumped back down into his seat, the small man leaned forward into the light. For a minute or so I couldn't place it, but I knew I had seen that face somewhere before, but where?

Then it hit me. The small man buying the drinks was the driver of Shagmar's big black stretch limo. But, why would Shagmar's driver be buying Barabbas drinks? Shagmar had promised me he would get Barabbas off my back, but a warning would have done that. So why was the driver spending three hours, and lots of dollars, getting Barabbas very drunk?

I didn't know the answer, and I couldn't waste time figuring it out. I finished my drink and made my way back to the office.

The mail had arrived—only a couple of bills. I checked the answer phone—only Mama wanting to know when I would be home for dinner. I pulled out my foolscap notepad, brought my case notes up to date, and slipped them into the Davidson file.

Just as I was putting the file away in my desk there was a gentle knock on my office door.

'Come in!' I called. 'It's not locked.'

My visitor was a small, thin, very elderly man. He wore an immaculately tailored dark blue double-breasted suit, a grey felt hat, and carried a silver-handled cane. 'Good afternoon,' he said, in a soft, precise, well educated voice.

I waved him to a seat.

'I am Lord Annas,' he explained.

'I've heard the name,' I said.

'Then you will know that I am a former high priest, and that Joseph Caiaphas, the present high priest, is my son-in-law.'

'Sure, I know all that.'

'And I know that you are currently employed by my son-in-law.'

'I'm not sure that I can discuss. . .'

'Your defence of your client's confidentiality is admirable, but misplaced. Caiaphas tells me everything. I am his principle adviser.'

'Then you know everything I know.'

'Precisely.'

'Then why are you here?'

'To press upon you more forcefully than I suspect my son-in-law has done the need for care and discretion and. . . success. . . in this matter.'

'Don't worry, he told me to be discreet.'

'But he is unlikely to have told you why.'

'He didn't go into a lot of details.'

'The responsibilities of his office weigh heavily upon him. He often hasn't the time to explain these things in detail. But I am retired now, and I have.'

'And you want to make sure I understand the big picture?'

'Precisely.'

'Well, that suits me fine. You talk and I'll listen.'

Lord Annas settled back in his chair and took a breath. 'This man whose corpse has vanished, and I speak to you now both as a priest and as a member of the noblest of the Sadducee families, this man is— the Enemy.'

He paused to let this sink in, then continued. 'During his lifetime he opposed us. He opposed not only our traditions but the stability and order of our nation. Are you taking this in, Mr Bartholomew? It is important.'

'I'm listening.'

'Do more than listen. Understand.'

He paused to collect his thoughts, then continued, 'We have come to an understanding with the Occupying Government. The size of his popular following threatened our stability. He was the Enemy.'

I raised my eyebrows, surprised by the quiet vitriol in his voice. He spoke of his 'enemy' in a tone of delicate disgust, like a cook removing a dead rat from the pantry.

'We have a system that runs smoothly,' he continued. 'All the gear wheels of our world turn together, and he was a threat to that. Did you know that he even opposed the markets we set up in the temple courtyard to sell sacrifices to pilgrims? He was an enemy of the free market economy!'

He paused again. His breathing had become laboured. He was an old man, and, I guessed, not a well one.

'We, the Sadducees, aided by the lawyers and the Pharisees, guide the life of our people through a delicate system of rules and regulations. With his bleeding heart compassion the Enemy threatened that whole system.'

Lord Annas took a large, white silk handkerchief out of his pocket and mopped his face. As he did so a whiff of eau-de-cologne wafted across the desk.

'Great and weighty matters hang upon the outcome of your investigation, Mr Bartholomew. The Enemy moved among the people telling his stories, teaching and healing. His following was large and excitable. A popular uprising by his supporters could have reduced this city to rubble. We had a responsibility to see that such a disaster was avoided. So we removed the Enemy the way a surgeon removes a cancer. Now, it is your job to cauterise the wound. If you fail, the wound will become infected.'

'Now you're confusing me. All this talk of surgeons and wounds. I'm a plain man, Lord Annas, talk to me plainly.'

He sniffed his scented handkerchief as though I was a bad odour. 'Very well then,' he said, 'plainly. If this man is not dead, if he has been delivered from the hands of death, then he is vindicated, and we...we...are...murderers.' The last word he hissed out, barely above a whisper.

He was as cold as a Frigidaire that old man. There was no trace of emotion as he continued. 'That must not happen. When we arrested our Enemy, his followers, even his closest followers, fled—which was what we were counting on. They dispersed. They were dispirited, disheartened. And our victory was complete. But once this story of a resurrection began to spread amongst them, well, all our good work began to fall apart. They started to regroup. Soon they will be as strong as ever they were. Perhaps stronger. They must be *stopped*!'

I nodded to show him that I was following his argument.

'You can stop them, Mr Bartholomew. Bring us the corpse of Jesus the Nazarene. We will hang his rotting carcass above the temple gate, and that will be the end of the Jesus Movement. For ever!'

Grasping his silver-handled cane he pushed himself to his feet. 'Perhaps now, Mr Bartholomew,' he said as he walked toward the door, 'you understand the great weight that rests upon your investigation. The stability of the administration rests upon it. Failure will be costly. Certainly costly for us. And we will ensure that it is costly for you too.'

He turned in the doorway to say, 'I bid you good afternoon, Mr Bartholomew,' and then he was gone.

I walked over to my window and stood, with my hands in my pockets, staring down into Coppersmith Street. I watched Lord Annas emerge from the alley that leads to my office and get into his car. It was a big old Peugeot, black with tinted windows. As his car crawled away through the crowded street I thought to myself, 'I admire his taste in wheels—those Gauls make good motor cars'.

Beneath my window the coppersmiths were bustling about under their awnings, hammering, gossiping, trading. It struck me that for a member of the aristocracy to come to this end of town was amazing. Lord Annas would have enjoyed visiting me about as much as he would enjoy holding a dinner party in a garbage dump. The Jesus Movement must really have them frightened.

Being caught in the middle of something that big made me uncomfortable and restless. I needed to think. And I think best when I'm walking. I looked at my watch, and decided it wasn't too early to start walking towards the office of Arimathea Industries.

Chapter 10

I walked along, lost in thought, oblivious to my surroundings. For all I noticed of the crowded city around me, I might as well have been walking through one of those Venetian pea-soupers.

Who stole the corpse? And why? Would the disciples of Jesus have been likely to steal the corpse if they were really defeated and frightened, as Lord Annas claimed? And if it wasn't them, who was it? And where was the corpse now?

I was roused from my reverie by a disturbance on the street ahead. A crowd had gathered around a noisy drunk. As I drew closer I could see that it was Barabbas, now drunker than ever.

'I'm a dead man walking,' he was roaring at the top of his lungs. 'Look at me! A dead man walking.' He started to swing his beefy arms about to keep the curious crowd at bay. Then there was some sort of disturbance and the big man staggered and fell onto the roadway—right in the path of an oncoming Lebanese timber truck. Women in the crowd screamed. Brakes screeched.

I pushed my way through the crowd, and saw that it was all over: Barabbas was dead, wedged under the wheels of the truck. There was nothing I could do. He had been a hood, but I felt sorry for him—he had died a desperately unhappy man.

As I backed away, I saw a man edging his way out of the crowd. It was Shagmar's driver. Now, that was interesting. Apparently he had been with Barabbas until the end so, did Barabbas fall under the wheels of that truck, or was he pushed? Had Shagmar decided that Barabbas was so obsessed with the death of Jesus that the only way to shut him up was to kill him?

Barabbas had claimed that he wanted Jesus forgotten, but, clearly, he could not himself forget. Barabbas seemed to be the saddest figure in the whole case.

I glanced at my watch—it was time for my appointment with Joseph Arimathea. I hailed a passing cab, and gave the cabbie the address.

As we neared the building I could make out the giant 'A.I.' sign revolving on the roof. The cab dropped me at the front door just at knock-off time. The big glass doors were open and hundreds of workers were streaming out. It was as though the building was flushing out its humans for the night.

I paid off the cab and jostled my way through the crowd: the middle-aged family men hurrying home; the young guys waiting for their girl friends; the old accountants pleased to be one day closer to retirement. None of them were worried about vanishing corpses, or religious fanatics, or hoods who threw themselves under the wheels of trucks. For a moment I envied them. But only for a moment. Nine-to-five just wasn't my scene. In a flock of a hundred sheep these were the ninety-nine who'd stay where they were put; I was the one who'd wander off exploring. Of course, I was more likely to be killed by a wolf, but that's the risk that goes with the territory.

The elevator shot me up to the twenty-fifth floor, where the secretary at the reception desk was expecting me. 'Just take a seat, Mr Bartholomew. Mr Arimathea won't keep you waiting long.'

She was one of those ice-cold blondes who know no fear. They know they are the doorkeepers to power, and they dispense justice, and occasionally mercy, from their reception desks as dispassionately as high court judges. If Tiberius Caesar had walked in, flanked by armed cohorts, she would have coolly said, 'Just take a seat, Mr Caesar. Mr Arimathea won't keep you waiting long.'

When the tall, oak door finally opened it was Arimathea himself who came out to meet me. 'Good afternoon, Mr Bartholomew,' he said, offering me his hand. 'Come into the office.'

He was not a tall man, a little below average height perhaps, with crinkly fair hair, a red complexion, and a smile as sunny as Santa Claus in the tropics.

Inside an office the size of a football field, he didn't take me to the quarter acre of oak that he called his desk, but led me to some armchairs grouped around a coffee table.

'We'll be more comfortable here,' he said. 'Would you like some coffee?'

'I never say "no" to coffee.'

The arctic blonde had followed us into the room. While she served the coffee Arimathea made small talk about the weather. When the door had clicked shut behind her, he got down to business. 'Now, Mr Bartholomew, what's your problem?' He was smiling as he said it, and it was the kind of smile that could have melted an iceberg.

This guy was going to be a problem. How could I confront him, and lean on him for the truth, if he was going to be so nice to me all the time?

'You buried the body of Jesus the Nazarene?'

'I don't deny that.'

'Why?'

'I don't want to appear rude, Mr Bartholomew, but is that any of your business?'

'Have you any reason for not telling me?'

'No, I haven't—not any more.'

'Well then?'

'You're not a reporter are you?'

'I'm exactly what I claim to be, Mr Arimathea.'

As I spoke I pulled out my wallet and flashed my P.I. licence at him. He leaned forward and checked me out against the photo on the licence.

'I hope you're not offended,' he said, 'but it's best to check.'

'You'd have to try harder than that to offend me. So, stop fencing with me: why did you bury Jesus Davidson?'

'Simple. Because, Mr Bartholomew, there was no one else to do it.'

'You were a follower of his?'

'Your use of the past tense is a mistake. I *am* a follower of his. In fact, more so now than before. When he was going around teaching I believed him. His words had the ring of truth about them. In fact, he was the very embodiment of truth. But I knew the establishment didn't like him, so I kept my opinions to myself. My company does a lot of business with the government and the temple. If we lost those contracts it would have been a major blow.'

'But now you're prepared to say what you really think?'

'Yes. I take no pride in admitting this to you, Mr Bartholomew. A man of honour should have the courage of his convictions, and I was not always entirely honourable, or entirely courageous.'

'But you've found the courage now?'

'Not "found"—it was a gift.'

'Yeah, sure. So who gave you the courage?'

'He did.'

'Pardon?'

'I was present at his trial on the Thursday night of Passover week. I'm a member of the temple council. Well, when I saw Davidson there, facing his accusers, so calm, so in control, so quietly courageous, I knew I had the courage to stand up for my beliefs.'

'So when he was condemned to death, you voted for acquittal?'

And then he blushed—the big, high-powered businessman actually blushed. 'Well, no. I should have. But all I did was abstain. It was not until the next day, when he was dying, and all his friends had deserted him, that I knew I had to do something. So, I went to His Excellency and asked for permission to bury the body.'

'Why did you need to go to the governor?'

'It was the Romans who conducted the execution, the remains were officially, legally, theirs.'

'Okay, so you saw this man who spoke the truth executed, and you decided to give him a decent burial?'

'If I hadn't his body would have been thrown on the city garbage dump.'

'I reckon you will have got the Caiaphas party off-side.'

'Oh, I lost some friends all right, no doubt about that.'

For a moment I sipped my coffee. I found this man's frankness plainly disconcerting. I took out my notebook, as I asked my next question. 'I presume you couldn't handle the burial alone—who helped you?'

'There's no harm in telling you, since the high priest and his party already know. It was a friend of mine who helped—Nicodemus, a lawyer. Nicodemus ben Gorion is his full name. He's been my lawyer for a long time, and he feels about the Nazarene the same as I do.'

As Arimathea remembered the burial he became restless. He stood up and walked over to the big tinted-glass window that formed the eastern wall of the office. He stood there for a minute in silence, his hands in his pockets, before he spoke.

'It really was,' he said, talking more to himself than to me, 'the strangest day of my life.'

Chapter 11

'Tell me about it.'

'Well... I'd had no sleep... depressed, and guilty, and I don't know what else, about the death penalty. All that Friday I just couldn't concentrate on work, so I went home and had lunch with my wife. But I was still restless, so after lunch I went for a walk.'

As he spoke he walked back across the office, and sat down facing me. 'I took a walk along the top of the city wall. Have you ever been up there? There's a six-foot-wide path behind the battlements. You'll often get a cool breeze there coming up the valley. But I'm so busy these days, I hadn't been there for years.'

'I guess you're like me—you think better when you're walking.'

His face lit up with one of those 'you-understand-me' looks. 'That's right. Anyway, when I'd been walking for half an hour or so, I came to the north wall. I wasn't conscious of deliberately walking in that direction, my feet just seemed to carry me there. Or maybe my mind was subconsciously steering me. I don't know. All I know is I found myself there. . . looking out on Skull Rock.'

'The execution site.'

'That's right.' He was looking down at the top of the coffee table, his fingers fiddling with a coaster as he continued. 'I could see it happening. Crucifixion is a brutal death. There were three of them altogether, dying slowly. Jesus was in the middle.'

He lifted his face. There were tears in his eyes. This tough businessman, wheeler-dealer, driver of hard bargains, takeover king, there were tears in his eyes.

'I saw him die,' he whispered.

I was embarrassed. I didn't want to watch a grown man cry. I picked up my notebook and doodled impatiently.

'And I realised,' said Arimathea, wiping his nose with a handkerchief and pulling himself together, 'that none of his followers were there. Well—very few of them. There was one young man and a few women. That's when I realised.'

'Realised what?'

'That they wouldn't be able to take care of the body. And I knew that I had to. But I needed help. So I went to my friend Nicodemus—we'd talked about Jesus and I knew how he felt. And he'd actually been stronger than me at the trial on the Thursday night—he'd stood up to the priests. All to no avail, of course. So, I went to see him.'

'And what did you two decide to do?'

'Well, Nicodemus said he'd get the burial spices and things to put in the tomb, and I said I'd call on the governor and ask for the body. I think I wanted to tackle the harder task to sort of make up for not taking a stand at the trial. And I rang my wife and asked her to put together a set of burial garments.'

'Then you went straight to the governor? And you were able to see him?'

'I had no trouble. He knows me, you see. We've met socially, and we've negotiated contracts.'

'You asked him to give you the body of Jesus? And he agreed?'

'Yes, he did. At first he was surprised that Jesus was already dead. In fact, he sent a messenger to check it out. But when the man came back and reported that Jesus really was, in fact, dead, he didn't seem to hesitate.'

'Didn't he seem surprised by your request?'

'A little. But not much. He knew that feelings were very mixed about Jesus. The temple syndicate wanted Jesus out of the way, but there were plenty of people who were neutral, and some who were supporters. I even got the feeling that the governor was quite happy at the thought that Jesus would get a decent burial. I suspect—I don't know, but I suspect—that he was not entirely happy about having to order the execution.'

'So you and Nicodemus took the body down to your rock tomb?'

'Yes. And we had to hurry. The sun was starting to set, and you know what the law is. We had to get the body into the tomb before the Sabbath started.'

'But you made it in time?'

'Oh, yes. But we didn't have time to do anything other than wrap the body in a shroud and lay it in the tomb. Just as we finished rolling the stone slate into place to seal the tomb, the sun set, and we both hurried back to our homes for the Sabbath.'

'Do you expect me to believe that two middle-aged businessmen were able to move that great stone? I've seen that stone, Mr Arimathea. It's very big and very heavy.'

'You're right. I know you're right—my muscles ached for twenty-four hours afterwards. But I still work out at the gym twice a week, and Nick is younger and fitter than I am. So we managed.'

'So whoever stole the corpse in the early hours of Sunday morning had to move that stone slab.'

'And that's the big question, isn't it, Mr Bartholomew? Who moved the stone?'

'When I can answer that, I'll be pretty close to finding the corpse.'

'That you will, Mr Bartholomew, that you will.' He was smiling when he said that, and there was a gleam in his eye of—I'm not sure what, but something. I had the feeling that he was saying more than the words appeared to mean.

'You don't happen to know who first found the tomb empty, do you?' I asked.

'Well, as I understand it, it was two or three of the women who had been at the execution.'

'What are their names?'

'I don't know them all, but they were led by Mary Magdalene.'

That name again. I'd missed her in Jerusalem, and it was now becoming vital that I track her down in Galilee.

At that moment the intercom on Arimathea's desk buzzed. 'I have to get back to work,' he said, standing up. 'I hope you'll excuse me.' And then he smiled again, and it was like seeing sunlight break through rainclouds.

We shook hands. He went to his desk and picked up his phone; I let myself out.

As I passed the receptionist I shot her a grin. 'Thanks for your help, sister,' I said. 'You've been swell.'

74

Her icy blue eyes shot an arctic blast at me that would have frozen a petrol fire. But I didn't care any more, I had seen my witness and got his story.

I should have gone back to the office, but I'm a weak man, so I ordered a cab and went to Nick's bar instead.

As I was paying off the cab I realised that I was hungry. When I took a look at the time I understood why.

'Good day?' asked Nick, as I propped myself against the bar.

'Strange day, Nick, old boy, very strange day.'

I ordered a light beer, and quietened my hunger with the snacks on the bar. After demolishing half a dozen dolmadas, and a fistful of black olives, and cubes of fetta cheese, I was feeling fuelled up and ready to start again.

'I knew I'd find you here,' boomed a voice behind me.

I turned around, and there was Sam Solomons, his bald head shining under the bright lights of the bar.

'I tried to ring your office,' said Sam. 'But you weren't in and you'd forgotten to switch on the answering machine. So I've had to come looking for you.'

'Sorry, Sammy, I'm always forgetting that damned machine. Did you get on to your contact at the barracks?'

'Of course I did! Do you doubt your old Sammy?'

'Never. What've you got?'

'It turns out that the captain on duty at the execution was a guy I've played poker with a couple of times. So, finish your drink and I'll take you over there, and introduce you. After the introduction I'll disappear. I don't want to mess in this case of yours, BB, I gather you're chasing a dead man.'

'Something like that.'

'And what with Eleazar blowing his brains out today, that whole Davidson business is back on the gossip circuit again. You'd heard about Eleazar, had you?'

'No,' I lied.

'Cops found him today. Out at his farm. Gun in his hand, brains all over the wall behind him. He was chief prosecution witness in the Davidson trial. So it sort of starts people talking again.'

Of course, what Sam didn't know but I did, was that Eleazar was also a secret agent of the syndicate who'd spent a long time trailing Davidson around the place.

'By the way,' said Sam, 'I've parked the Landrover in front of your office. Here are the keys. Just bring it back in one piece, okay?'

'Sammy. . .you know me.'

'That's what I'm worried about. Finish your drink and I'll take you to meet the captain.'

Chapter 12

Captain Marcus Longhinus had rooms in the non-commissioned officers' quarters in the north-east of the city, not far from the Fortress Antonia. Before leaving Nick's bar I had the forethought to arm myself with a bottle of imported Gaelic whisky.

Sam Solomons led me up a narrow, winding staircase, at the top of which he knocked on a heavy wooden door. It was opened by a solidly built, straight-backed man with a weathered face, grey hair, and a military moustache.

'Good evening, Captain,' said Sam. 'Do you remember me? Sam Solomons. We've played poker together.'

'No sir, we have not played poker together. You have beaten me at poker and won a great deal of money off me! It's nice to see you again, Sammy. Step inside.'

We followed the captain inside. His sitting room was sparsely but comfortably furnished.

'Marcus, this is my friend Ben Bartholomew.'

'Pleased to meet you, sir. Any friend of Sammy's is a friend of mine. Take a seat the both of you.'

'I'm afraid I can't stay,' said Sammy. 'The fact is, Marcus, I've brought Ben here because he thought you might be able to help him.'

Marcus Longhinus frowned, so I jumped in quickly and said, 'Three weeks ago, on a Friday afternoon, you were in charge of an execution party. I just want to talk to you about it, that's all.'

As I spoke I produced the bottle of whisky. The captain's eyes lit up like full moons when he saw it. 'And what a pleasant way you have of talking,' he said, 'I'll fetch the glasses.'

As the Roman captain rummaged in a cupboard, Sammy said, 'I really must be going, Marcus. I'll catch you later, Ben.' And with that he was gone.

'Take a seat, sir, take a seat,' said the captain, returning with the glasses and waving me towards the dining room table. I handed him the whisky, he poured, and we sat down. 'Now, how can I help you?'

'As I said, it's about that execution party.'

'There were two common thieves and one political prisoner. . .'

'That's right. And it's the political prisoner I'm interested in, one Jesus Davidson. His corpse has vanished from the rock tomb in which it was buried.'

'So, the gossip is true then?'

'And I've been hired to find it.'

'Who by?'

'The temple authorities.'

He snorted. 'A bunch of jackals. I wouldn't give them the time of day.'

'I'm not saying I don't agree with you. But I can't afford to pick and choose my clients. I'm just trying to earn an honest living.'

'Oh, I don't hold you responsible for your clients, sir, have no fear of that.'

'Well, the execution then. What do you remember?'

'About Jesus Davidson?'

'Yes.'

'I can tell you this, sir, he died like a man. He had grit, sir, real grit. I've seen some men, big tough brutes some of them, whimper like babies on those crosses. But not this Jesus. He took his punishment like a man.'

He poured himself another whisky and then added, 'In fact, I'll go further than that. He stood up to the pain like a soldier, and you can't say better than that.'

'Indeed you can't,' I said, agreeing quickly.

'You know, right up until the last minute or two there was not a word of complaint out of him, not a single word. Which is more than can be said for the other two we had that day.'

'And did all three of them die before sunset?'

'That they did, sir. That they did. The two thieves I was not surprised at. But the one in the middle . . . well . . . I rather expected him to last a little longer. He might even have taken two or three days in dying—some of them do, you know. He looked tough to me. Not big, but wiry. He had the build of a tradesman, or maybe a farmer. He'd worked hard, and been out in the sun, you could see that. And there was life in his eyes. I can tell you, sir, that I have never seen more life in a man's eyes than I saw in his eyes that day.'

'I'm surprised he looked so fit to you. I thought he had been tortured by the time he got to the execution site.'

'That's true. Yes, he had. But I've seen a lot of executions, sir, and my judgement is not too bad, even if I say so myself. And underneath the blood and the sweat I could see his toughness.'

'One other thing, when it was all over, are you quite sure that he was dead?'

'Sure? Of course, I'm sure! Do you think we Romans are backyard amateurs? When it comes to executions, we are experts. When we execute people they are finished, done, polished off, deceased, defunct, passed on, departed, croaked, conked out, perished, pegged out, kicked the bucket in a word—dead.'

He took a sip from his glass, lingered over it for a moment, then continued, 'Let me tell you, sir, I have seen many executions. I haven't kept count, but there must have been hundreds. I know when a man's dead, I'm an expert, and Jesus was dead. I'd stake my stripes on it. Come to think of it, I did stake my stripes on it. If I made a mistake like that I'd lose my stripes, and end up in the guardhouse myself.'

'No chance he could have fallen into a deep faint and recovered later?'

'What? And walked out of his own tomb? Is that what you're thinking?'

'Well . . .'

'Forget it! You didn't see his wounds, I did. There was no way he was walking anywhere. But if you want to check up for yourself I'll give you the name and address of the doctor who signed the death certificate. Go and talk to him, he'll tell you the same thing.'

Out of his pocket he dug a scrap of paper and a stub of pencil, and wrote down a name and address. The name was Dr Titus Theophilus.

'As you can see,' said the captain, 'he's a Greek, and Greeks make the best doctors. You go and speak to the doc and he'll confirm what I've told you.'

'In that case, there's one other thing . . . At the

execution itself, were any of his followers hanging about? Was there any conversation—I guess what I'm looking for are signs of a conspiracy—any hint of a plan to steal the corpse?'

'Only a bunch of women, that's all—oh, and one youngster. And they were all in tears. The whole bang lot of them. The only thing they were conspiring to do was to break their hearts. They must have loved him—you could see that.'

He leaned across the table and said in a low voice, 'His mother was one of them. I'm not a soft man, but I don't like to see their mothers in tears'.

I got up and shook his hand. 'Thank you, Captain,' I said, 'you've been a great help.'

Out in the street the night had turned cold and I turned up my collar. It was little more than a narrow alleyway, but at least it had no twists and turns because it followed the wall of the fortress. Because it was so straight, and because the moon had come out, I easily picked up the shadow that was following me.

I could just hear the shuffle of feet, and took a quick glance behind me. The barest flicker of movement told me I was being tailed.

I was walking quickly, but he was gaining on me. If he was just going to follow me, I was confident I could lose him later, in the middle of town. But if he had something more violent in mind, he'd be sure to strike before I got to the bright lights.

I increased my pace. But so did he. He was still gaining on me. I could see the end of the alley, but it looked a long way off. I decided to make a sprint for it.

I began to run, my legs pumping, my lungs sucking air. My shadow broke into a run behind me. He abandoned his cover and sprinted after me. But I was quicker. Almost at once I was putting distance between us.

The end of the alleyway was close. I eased off a little, knowing he couldn't catch me. But he knew he didn't have to. As I passed the third house from the end of the alley a large figure stepped out of the shadows. I was going too fast to stop. I collided with him. It was like hitting concrete.

The big leather-jacketed man I had run into, twisted me into an armlock before I could stop him. I didn't have the breath, or the energy to struggle.

My pursuer caught up with us. I was pleased to hear him gasping for air while he fumbled in his pocket. He pulled out a flashlight and flicked it on.

My captors were the two RIA men who had been in my office in the morning.

'Hi fellas,' I wheezed.

My pursuer was Mr Charming, and his silent friend was the man who had held me pinioned from behind.

Chapter 13

Once Mr Charming had caught his breath he pulled a forty-five calibre automatic out of a shoulder holster and pointed it straight at my chest. 'You can let him go now,' he said to his silent partner.

'Thanks,' I said, flexing my sore arm. 'But why have I been grabbed? I thought I'd come to an understanding with you guys?'

'Someone important wants to speak to you.'

'I see...and this is the invitation I can't refuse?'

'Exactly. That's enough talking. Get a move on,' he said, gesturing with his gun.

The silent partner led the way, I followed, and Mr Charming and his gun brought up the rear.

I was taken back down the alley and around the corner. We kept going until we came to a long, high, plastered wall. The wall was blank except for a single heavy wooden door. One of my RIA guards knocked on the door. A small panel in the door opened, our identities were checked, and, without a word being spoken, the door was unbarred and we were allowed inside.

Once inside we crossed a courtyard, then entered another door. There was no moonlight, and only one dim light-bulb burning in the courtyard. Beyond the second door was a long corridor. It too was dimly lit. A narrow flight of stairs led to another long, narrow corridor. As we walked I was trying to get my sense of direction working, to calculate where I was. A double doorway let us into a broader, better lit corridor. And then I worked out where I was.

'We're in Government House, aren't we?'

Mr Charming just poked me in the back with his gun and said, 'Keep walking.'

But even without his confirmation I knew I was right. I had been brought into Government House through a back entrance.

After walking for what felt like miles I was led into an office, a large, cedar-panelled office, book-lined, with thick carpet, leather-covered armchairs, a marble fireplace, and a vast desk of polished oak.

The silent partner pushed me into a chair, then walked over and pressed a small electric button that was inset into the desk. Both RIA men then retired to an inconspicuous corner, but I noticed that they both still kept their eyes on me.

After a wait of several minutes the double doors behind the desk swung open. As they did so Mr Charming snapped, 'Stand up, Bartholomew.' I stood up.

A small man walked into the room and Mr Charming announced, 'Your Excellency, this is Mr Bartholomew. Bartholomew, you have the honour to meet His Excellency Pontius Pilate, Governor of Judaea.'

'Sit, Mr Bartholomew, sit,' said the governor. Not much over five feet, he was wearing a uniform of dark green, with a broad leather belt, and leather boots that almost reached his knees. I knew, all Jerusalem knew, that the governor was inordinately fond of uniforms, and wore them most of the time. His chest shone with brass buttons on the uniform and three rows of impressive looking medals. Of course, most of the medals he had awarded to himself.

'Thank you for responding so promptly to my invitation, Mr Bartholomew,' he said as he paced back and forth on the luxurious carpet, adding, 'Sit down, sit down. I can't talk to you unless you sit down.'

I realised that the only way the governor could look down on me was if I sat down, so I sat down.

Pilate didn't, he kept pacing back and forth. 'You Jews are very difficult people to govern, Mr Bartholomew, did you realise that?' he said.

'Well, I—'

'Don't apologise,' Pilate interrupted. (I had no intention of apologising!) 'I like it. I like the fact that you're hard to govern. I like a challenge. I respond to a challenge. Now, if you were as easy to govern as the Syrians I would find that very dull. And I like you Jews, did you realise that?'

'Well, I—'

'Don't contradict me. It's true. I know you might not believe it, but it's true. I like you Jews. You've got pride, and grit, and you're prepared to fight to defend your traditions. I like that in a people. I admire it. But it doesn't lead to an easy or comfortable relationship between the governor and the people. You'd admit that, wouldn't you?'

'Well, I—'

'Of course, you would! I mean to say, just look back at some of the struggles we've had together. And you notice I don't say "Some of the struggles I've had with

you"? Oh no, I say, "The struggles we've had together."
Because that's the way it really is. It's all a matter of
a governor and a people struggling to come to know
each other, to discover how to work with each other.
That's right, isn't it?'

'Well, I—'

'I knew you'd agree with me. We think alike, don't
we, Mr Bartholomew? Maybe that's why I've had these
little clashes in my time here, because you Jews think
the same way I do. Do you remember what happened
when I first arrived, Mr Bartholomew?'

'Well—'

'That's right. I had the legions march up from the
coast, bearing their regimental standards. And when
they arrived at Jerusalem I had the standards brought
into the city so that the sign of the Roman Eagle would
fly over Jerusalem. And what happened?'

'Well—'

'I was as popular as a pork chop at a Jewish
barbecue, that's what happened! All hell broke loose.
You people carried on as though any image that might
suggest the Divine Emperor Tiberius was some sort
of sacrilege. For six days there was this wonderful
tussle of wills between me and your Jewish leaders.
And then, after six days, I decided I had tested them
enough and I had the standards taken back to
Caesarea on the coast. And you know why, don't you?'

'Was it—'

'It was what I had always intended to do, that's why.
I was just testing you people out, just getting your
measure, that's all. That's the sort of thing a new
governor has to do. But there was a complicating
factor. Can you guess what the complicating factor
was, Mr Bartholomew?'

'Well—'

'It was diplomacy, Mr Bartholomew. I'm a plain, bluff military man, and I had given no thought to the niceties of diplomacy. It turned out that the report that was sent back to Rome by diplomatic courier was a gross misinterpretation of what had actually happened. And the message got to the Senate. Well, you know what the Senate are, don't you?'

'Ah—'

'A bunch of old women, that's what! And they sent me a message: "No more nationalistic uprisings," they said. "Put a bit more *pax* in the *pax romana*," they said. As if they'd know anything, hundreds of miles away from the action. Unfortunately, by the time their message had reached me we'd had the little matter of the temple funds. But I'd taken the temple funds for a good reason, hadn't I?'

'Well—'

'To build an aqueduct! That's why! Everywhere we go we Romans build aqueducts. It's our thing. It's one of our trade marks. We bring Roman civilisation to the places we conquer. And that means things like aqueducts, and roads, and Fiats, and pizzas, and dry cleaning fluid! That's civilisation! Isn't civilisation wonderful, Mr Bartholomew?'

'I guess—'

'And just because I was using temple funds to build this wonderful aqueduct, there was another howl of complaint from you Jews. You're fussy people, you really are. And you make life hard for a governor. But I've learned how to play you people now, and there won't be any more complaints going back to the Senate, or to the emperor. And that's where you come in, isn't it, Mr Bartholomew?'

'How—'

'I signed the execution order for this Jesus

Davidson. Caiaphas assured me that the man was a problem. I would have let him go. I was quite happy to let him go. But Caiaphas wanted him dead, and I didn't want another complaining telegram going to Rome. So I agreed. You see my position, don't you?'

'Well—'

'I knew you would. Now Caiaphas is panicking that the Jesus Movement may not be under control. Your job, so I have been told, is to find the evidence that will destroy the movement. How are you doing?'

'Well, I have—'

'Good. I'm pleased to hear that you're doing well. You have an excellent reputation. I have every faith in you. But whatever you do for Joe Caiaphas, Mr Bartholomew, there's something I want you to do for me. Can you guess what it is?'

'Ah—'

'That's right! I knew you'd understand. I have only one requirement from you: no political trouble. If any evidence you find looks like stirring up a political hornet's nest, lose it. If you come across any signs of nationalistic fervour, hose it down. If the political temperature starts to rise, cool it. You are my window into this Jesus situation, Mr Bartholomew. And I don't care what result you come up with, as long as there are no more complaining telegrams going to Rome.'

Pilate walked over to where I was sitting and leaned over me. Up close I could see the Bolognese sauce stains on the front of his uniform. Romans may have invented dry cleaning fluid, but Pilate didn't use the stuff too often.

'No political trouble, Mr Bartholomew,' said Pilate, leaning over me. 'Anything else you like, but no political trouble.'

He straightened up and clicked his fingers at the two RIA men.

'Take him away,' he said.

In a moment they were at my side and marching me out of the room.

Chapter 14

I was taken out to the corridor, and back down the way we had come. We had gone no more than a few yards when a door on our right flew open and a woman stepped out.

She was middle-aged, good looking in a blousy sort of way, but overdressed and over-made-up. Judging from the wild and vacant look in her eyes, if she had been doing anything with dry cleaning fluid, she had been drinking it.

'Bring him in here,' she commanded.

With only a moment's hesitation, my two guards wheeled me into her room. It was a sort of sitting room, and, like her, was overdecorated.

'Now, leave us alone,' she said.

'But, Lady Claudia,' protested Mr Charming, 'we can't do that. It would be more than our lives are worth if your husband ever found out.'

'He won't. And it's only for a few minutes.'

'If you insist...'

'I do.'

Mr Charming shrugged his shoulders. He frisked me, took the revolver out of my shoulder holster, and then he and his silent partner left the room. I had no doubt that they would be standing guard just outside the door.

'Do you know who I am?' asked the woman, turning to me.

Before I could answer she said, 'I am the governor's wife. And I wanted to talk to you, because I heard what my husband said to you. I always leave my connecting door ajar. I did the night he came, and that's how I knew what was happening.'

'The night who came?' I asked.

'Oh, that odious high priest man—Joseph Caiaphas. But coming at night was most unusual. He's never done it before or since. Just that night.'

As she spoke she paced back and forth, twisting her hands restlessly around each other. I glanced around her room. The furniture and furnishings were all chintz and lace. There was a big astrological chart hanging on the wall, several packs of tarot cards on the coffee table. That told me a lot about Lady Claudia: whatever else she was, she was a nut.

'It was a few weeks ago,' she continued, 'on a Thursday night. During that last big festival thing.'

'Passover,' I volunteered.

'Whatever it's called,' she said. 'Anyway, that awful man called to see Ponty quite late at night. And, of course, I listened. Well, it seemed he had a prisoner, or was about to arrest a prisoner, and wanted Ponty to agree to confirm a death penalty first thing the next morning.'

She picked up a piece of polished crystal from the coffee table, and fiddled with it nervously as she continued to pace and talk.

'Of course, Ponty didn't want any more political trouble. He is trying terribly hard to get on with these silly people. But it's very hard. They are sensitive about the silliest things. Do you know who my grandfather was?'

I shrugged my shoulders.

'Augustus, that's who!' she said, with a note of triumph. 'Caesar Augustus. I am a grand-daughter of Caesar Augustus. What do you think of that?'

'Noble,' I said. (Well, what else could I say?)

'Well put. Yes, I am noble. I am positively stinking with nobility. And when I wanted to have a look inside that temple the silly people here wouldn't let me. Well, I may be a Gentile, and a woman, but I am a noblewoman—a Roman noblewoman. And they still wouldn't let me. Ponty told me to stop nagging about it, and I'm a very good wife so I did stop nagging. But it bothered me. And do you know why I wanted to see inside their silly temple?'

'Tell me.'

'I will tell you. Because there were emanations! What do you think of that!'

'Emanations?'

'Exactly. I'm a sensitive, you see. Back in Rome, my clairvoyant said I was one of the most sensitive people she had ever met. I pick up the vibrations of places, you see. And people. I am aware of ethereal emanations to which others are simply deaf. And Ponty trusts my sensitivity. On several occasions I have had clairvoyant flashes that have been quite helpful to him. I'm not often wrong. You see?'

'I see.'

'The emanations from the temple were particularly strong. So I was bothered when I couldn't see inside. And I was puzzled by Caiaphas. I mean, he ran that temple place, but there were no emanations from him, oh no, none at all. He didn't have a single vibration in him. How could a man function so close to such a powerful source and not emanate at all?'

'I don't know.'

'Neither do I. It had me quite puzzled. I decided in the end that he was just blind and deaf to the astral plane, that's all. And he came here, very late at night, wanting an agreement to a death penalty on a charge, he said, of blasphemy. Well, I asked myself, how could anybody who is spiritually dead meat know anything about blasphemy? And the man he wanted killed, Jesus Davidson, I'd heard about. Nothing but good reports. So I went to bed that night quite troubled, you see?'

'I see.'

'And all that night I had nightmares. All night. I woke up in the middle of the night with a terrible one, and I had to get up and get myself a little drink. I often need a little drink in the middle of the night to get back to sleep. And when I went back to sleep, I had another nightmare—worse than the first! It was terrible.'

'I'm sure it was.'

'When I woke up it was dawn. Well, only just dawn, that first grey light, you know?'

'I know.'

'And Ponty was already up. I realised that he had gone down to confirm that death penalty that Caiaphas wanted confirmed. Well, I sat down and scribbled out a quick note telling Ponty that I'd had a really powerful flash that Ponty should refuse to have anything to do with this Davidson. That's what I wrote. And I sent that note down with my maid, and I had a little drink, just to settle myself down, you understand.'

'Of course.'

'And then I went to relax in my bath. Well, imagine my horror when later, over breakfast, Ponty told me he hadn't been able to release Davidson. He'd tried, he said, but Caiaphas had been too clever. Accused Davidson of political things, instead of blasphemy. Hinted heavily there would be another complaining telegram going to Rome unless Ponty kept his end of the agreement. So, Ponty couldn't get out of it. I was very upset, very upset indeed. It was worse than the temple business. When you're a sensitive you feel these things, you see.'

'I see.'

'And now it's all blown up again, and I'm very worried. There are dark emanations on the astral plane, Mr Bartholomew, very dark emanations. And I don't want any of them to touch Ponty. Or me, for that matter. Are you a sensitive, Mr Bartholomew?'

'Not very, I'm afraid.'

'Oh, dear me, that is a problem. I want you to promise me that you'll try to be aware of the spiritual plane, Mr Bartholomew. You must take great care that nothing you do makes the spiritual aura worse. Will you promise me that, Mr Bartholomew?'

'I'll try, but—'

'Don't treat it lightly, Mr Bartholomew. There are forces and powers in play here that we know so little about.'

Before I could reply the door opened and my RIA guards came back into the room.

'That will have to be all, Lady Claudia,' said Mr Charming. 'We can't leave him here any longer.'

And with that I was whisked back out into the corridor, and marched briskly along the way I had come. At the back door my gun was returned to me,

I was thrust out into the street, and the door was closed and barred behind me.

As I slipped the gun back into its holster I thought about the governor's wife and her 'emanations'. This surely was one weird case.

Chapter 15

That night I had difficulty sleeping. It wasn't that I was plagued with Lady Claudia's nightmares. Nothing like that. I was restless, that's all. I guess the case was getting me down. At any rate, as the first faint flush of dawn lit up my bedroom window, I decided that I was so wide awake it was silly to just lie there thinking. So I got dressed, went downstairs, and got myself some bagels and coffee.

What I needed was to get out of the house—otherwise I'd just prowl around until I woke up my parents. And at their age they need their sleep. Come to think of it, at my age I need my sleep. But if I couldn't sleep I might as well think.

I let myself quietly out of the house, and there stood Sam's old Landrover. That gave me an idea. I would drive to the execution spot—Skull Rock. It was just out of town, and at this time of the morning it would be quiet and deserted. I wanted to see the place where Jesus died and being there might help me to focus my thoughts.

The Landrover started on the first kick. I eased it into gear, and drove off slowly enough to keep the old rattletrap quiet.

I drove through the deserted streets in the cold grey light of early dawn towards the north-west quarter of the city, out of the city through the Fish Gate and then turned right along the road that wound around outside the city wall. I brought the Landrover to a halt at the foot of the hill the Romans used as an execution site.

It was clear how the place had got its nickname. The flat rocky side of the hill that faced the city had shallow indentations that resembled the nose and eye sockets in a skull. I left the Landrover at the base of the hill, found a place where the slope was not so steep, and scrambled up to the peak. There I found another reason for the 'Skull Rock' nickname: it was littered with broken bone fragments—remnants of earlier Roman executions.

In front of me were the slots cut into the rock to hold the wooden crosses. There were no crosses there, of course. The Romans kept re-using the same crosses to save on the cost of carpentry. Around the slots were black stains which spread across the rock. I knew what they were—dried blood.

Just then the sun broke through the early morning cloud. The eerie yellow light glinted on a piece of metal, and I bent to pick it up. It was a ten-inch iron spike, now gone rusty with blood—the kind of spike the Romans used to nail the victims onto their crosses.

Suddenly behind me there was the sound of sandals crunching on gravel. I froze. Who else would be visiting Skull Rock at the crack of dawn?

The visitor came up the slope towards me with the sun behind him, and for a minute he was nothing but a black outline against the liquid gold of the rising sun. When I could make out his face I was relieved to see that it was the Captain—Marcus Longhinus!

'Morning, Captain,' I said.

'Who's there?' he snapped as I stood up. 'Oh, it's you, sir. I am surprised to find you pursuing your investigations so early in the morning.'

'Oh, I couldn't sleep, Captain, so I thought I might as well work. What about you? Did you also have difficulty sleeping?'

'Oh, ah. Yes, I see what you mean. It does look a little odd, doesn't it? Well. . .you see, sir. . . I've rather got into the habit of coming out here in the mornings, over the past few weeks.'

'Why?'

'I come here to think, sir, that's why.'

'Now, that's interesting, Captain. That's why I came here this morning—to find a quiet place to think.'

'But, there's more to it than that, isn't there, sir? I mean to say, there are lots of quiet places.'

'Yes, you're right, of course. It's this Jesus Davidson business—I wanted to see where he died. And what about you, Captain, what's your reason for coming here to do your thinking?'

For a moment he looked down at the ground and shuffled his feet. Then he said, 'Just like yourself, sir—it's this Davidson business.'

'I don't understand.'

'We, not having been here that day, you wouldn't. But I was, see. And ever since, his death has haunted me.'

'But you must have seen a great many deaths, Captain?'

'I've seen hundreds, sir, hundreds. But none like this.'

'Tell me about it. It might help.'

We sat down together on a large boulder, and it was clear from the Captain's face that he welcomed having someone to tell about the death that haunted him.

'Well, it was a Friday, sir, the day before the Jewish Sabbath, and that always makes executions a bit difficult. A bit hurried, if you know what I mean. I had a detail of four men on execution duty that day. All experienced men. They'd done this sort of thing often before. The prisoner escort detail arrived with the three prisoners about 9 o'clock in the morning. The two criminals had come fresh from prison, one was quiet and white with fear, the other was struggling and swearing. The third man...'

'Jesus?'

'...Yes, Jesus, had been beaten that morning and was in considerable pain. His back was still bleeding from a whipping he'd had, and some idiot had woven a sort of coronet thing out of thorn branches and pushed it onto his head. I'm a hard man, sir, but that sort of stupid cruelty makes me angry.

'Anyway we had them up on their crosses by a few mintues after nine. I always make the detail move fast with that. Nailing the hands and feet to the timber is the worst part, for us as well as for them, so it's best to get it done as quickly as possible. If you see what I mean?'

I nodded, and he continued.

'My men divided up the clothes and personal property of the victims amongst themselves—it's one of the perks of the job—and after that it was just a matter of waiting. There were some of Davidson's friends and relatives there, only a few, actually, and mostly women. During the morning they didn't come too close. And there were a few priests, mostly young ones, shouting insults at Davidson, and, of course, there are always some curious onlookers. You always get that. At a construction site or a crucifixion, I always say, you'll always get the curious wanting to stop and have a look. And then there was an eclipse of the sun. You remember that?'

'Yes. I was up in Jericho that day, but I remember the eclipse.'

'Well, that started about noon and kept us in darkness, or a sort of grey twilight, until 3 o'clock in the afternoon. By then most of the priests and the idlers had drifted away. That was when Davidson's friends came closer and spoke to him, and he, I think, spoke to them.'

'Did you hear what they said?'

'No, I wasn't close enough. After a while his friends moved back a bit. They were in tears, of course, and just couldn't stand to see him...like that. Well, the crowd had gone, the friends had moved back, my men weren't close—they were sitting over to one side gambling—so I walked up to him.'

'Up to Jesus?'

'Yes. I stood right at the foot of his cross, the middle one it was. And then there was an earthquake. Not a big one. Just a small shudder. Then he said something. Almost a whisper it was, but I heard it quite clearly. "It is finished," he said. Then his body sort of heaved and shuddered and he fell limp against the cross. He was dead.'

The Captain stopped and turned his face away. After he'd taken a couple of deep breaths he continued.

'A while later Pilate sent up a couple of guards to order us to finish these people off. The Jews didn't want them hanging there on the Sabbath, so they had to be dead and cut down by sunset. The two criminals were still alive, so I sent my corporal to break their legs. That always finishes them in a few minutes. But with the other one—with Jesus Davidson—I pointed out that he was already dead. The corporal stuck a spear in his side to make sure I was right. He rammed the spear a good way in, and a mixture of blood and water gushed out. There was no doubt that Jesus was dead. So then we cut down the three bodies.'

The Captain got up and walked over to the edge of the flat rocky summit of the hill. He stood there for a moment, staring towards the city, then he turned around and said to me, 'He was a good man, sir. A good man. A righteous man. Why would they want to get rid of a man like that?'

'I don't know, Captain, I just don't know.' (Remembering my conversation with Lord Annas, I thought: 'I do know, but it's none of my business.')

Chapter 16

Captain Longhinus and I walked down the hill together, and I gave him a lift back into town. We travelled in silence, each preoccupied with his own thoughts.

I dropped the Captain at the Fortress Antonia, and went in search of Dr Titus Theophilus.

He had a surgery nearby in the market quarter, so I found a place to prop the car, and to fill in some time before the surgery opened, I stopped to have a second breakfast of raisin toast and orange juice.

As I sipped my juice I tried to put some of the pieces of the puzzle together. What the Captain had told me was interesting, but it didn't get me anywhere. Where was the corpse of Jesus the Nazarene? Who had taken it from the sealed rock tomb in the garden? Certainly not ordinary grave-robbers—not when there were soldiers on guard. I know the professional thieves of Jerusalem; it's my job to know them. If they spot a Roman soldier on guard they'll go find an easier mark. Anyway there was nothing of value to a thief in the tomb. And I was pretty certain that the Romans didn't take it, or the temple officials. That only left the Davidson crowd—his disciples—or, Jesus himself. As Shagmar had suggested, perhaps the man hadn't died on the cross. Perhaps he'd fainted and revived in the cool of the tomb. That was what I was about to check out.

The clock on the town hall chimed the half hour—half past eight. I decided to try the doctor's place.

His waiting room door had one of those little bells on a spring that tinkled when it opened. There were already three patients ahead of me. I picked up an old copy of the weekly *Tempus* and settled down to wait.

After about half an hour Dr Theophilus ushered me into his surgery. He was a short, bald guy with a fussy manner.

'And what seems to be the problem, young man?' he asked.

'I don't have a physical problem—'

'Apart from lack of sleep.'

'How could you tell?'

'I used my eyes. Now, if you don't have a physical problem, what can I do for you?'

I pulled out my licence and flashed it at him. 'Answer a few questions,' I said.

'A Private Detective,' he muttered. 'I've never met a Private Detective before. Well, pay me a consultation fee, and I'll answer your questions. What do you want to know?'

'There were three executions on the Friday of Passover week,' I said, as the first denarius rattled on to the desk.

'Yes, I remember.'

'Two criminals, and a political prisoner named Jesus Davidson. You signed all three death certificates.'

'No argument so far. What about it?'

'The body of Jesus has gone missing.'

'Well I didn't take it! I know there are some surgeons who do that sort of thing, but I'm a physician and I didn't touch his body. At least, not after it was buried I didn't.'

'No one's saying you did.'

'Well then...?'

'I've got to explore every possibility. Are you sure that Jesus was dead when you signed the death certificate?'

'Is that what this is all about? Of course he was dead! You'd find livelier people in the town cemetery! When you're about to be crucified you don't start making plans for the future. Crucifixion is fatal, you know, quite fatal.'

'No chance of a mistake?'

'Do I look like an idiot?'

'No chance that he just fainted and revived later in the coolness of the tomb?'

'Look, like all doctors I may bury my mistakes, but I don't bury them until they're dead. When Roman soldiers are told to execute someone, they execute them. They don't muck about. And when they show me a crucified body that's stopped breathing, I sign a death certificate. In my long medical experience there are not a lot of people walking about who've stopped breathing.'

'Okay, Doc, don't get your toga in a knot, I've got to ask.'

'Let me ask you a question, young man: do you know what kills the victims of crucifixion?'

'Medically speaking?'

'Yes, medically speaking.'

'No...I guess not.'

'Then let me tell you. They die from asphyxiation. Sure they're suffering from exhaustion, exposure, and physical collapse, but in the end what kills them is asphyxiation. You see, when they're first hung up on a cross they support their weight with their arms and legs, but as the pain increases and exhaustion sets in they sag forward. In the end this causes a complete collapse of the lung cavity and they asphyxiate.'

'So, as their body weight sags down, they can't expand their lungs, so they can't breathe and they die?'

'Precisely. That's why they sometimes break their legs to speed up death—it makes it impossible for them to support their own weight, their body collapses downwards, and they asphyxiate in a few minutes.'

'But Jesus was already dead, wasn't he? And it was unnecessary to break his legs.'

'As I recall, you are correct. But let me check my records.'

He left his desk and went to an old filing cabinet. After a few minutes hunting he pulled out an oblong, white card.

'Ah, here we are. It says here that the legs were not broken, and a spear in the side was used to guarantee death.'

'Marcus Longhinus told me that blood and water flowed out when the spear went in—what does that mean?'

'Well, I wasn't there when the corporal stuck the spear in the side of the corpse, but I saw the wound afterwards. In my opinion he was suffering from acute dilation of the stomach, and the spear wound drew watery fluid from the stomach, and blood from the heart and great vessels of the thorax. Needless to say, young man, such a wound would be instantly fatal if the victim was not already dead, which, in this case, he obviously was.'

I thanked Dr Theophilus for his help, and left. It was clear that whatever else Jesus did on the cross, he most certainly died. Despite Shagmar's having raised it, it was always an unlikely possibility. But it's always good to rule out each possibility—even the unlikely ones.

I left the Landrover where I had parked it and walked back towards the barracks district.

It was becoming more obvious that there could be only one solution to the disappearance of the corpse— the one that Caiaphas had suggested when he briefed me: the disciples had stolen it. But which of them? And when? And where had they hidden the corpse?

The place to start finding answers to these questions was with the young Roman soldier who had been on guard on the night the corpse vanished. Shagmar had told me that the guard, Magnus Cassius by name, was having a nervous breakdown. And so had his landlady, Mrs Goldblum. Perhaps his breakdown was related to something that happened on the night the corpse vanished?

The alleyway containing widow Goldblum's house was so narrow that I could almost have touched both sides with my outstretched arms. I knocked on the door and waited. And waited. I could hear noises inside, but I had to knock again—louder—before the door opened. And then it only opened a few inches.

'Mrs Goldblum?'

'Oh, it's you again.' The door swung slowly open, and I stepped inside. She stood back to let me enter. Disapproval was written all over Mrs Goldblum's face.

'He's upstairs,' she said in a sour voice. 'Don't talk to him for too long, he's not well.'

I started up the narrow, dark staircase.

'And don't get him excited,' she called after me. 'It's not good for him.'

Chapter 17

At the head of the stairs was a plain, wooden door. I knocked and pushed it open. Inside was a small bedroom with a single window. The shutters were closed, and the room was dark and gloomy. Against the far wall was a single bed, apart from which the room was almost bare—just a chest, a wooden stool, and a small table carrying a water jug and a cup.

I stepped into the room and banged the door shut behind me. The pile of crumpled bed clothes stirred, and a tousled head emerged. He was very young, maybe nineteen, pale, pasty-faced, and unshaven.

'Morning, Magnus,' I said.

'You Bartholomew?' he asked, in a croaky voice.

'That's me. Your friendly, neighbourhood detective.'

He pushed back the covers and propped himself up into a sitting position. 'What do you want?'

'You were on duty at the tomb of Jesus Davidson on Sunday morning the ninth of April.'

'So what?'

'Were you the only guard?'

'No there were two of us.'

'Who was the other?'

'Julius Publius.'

'Where can I find him?'

'He's. . .he's. . .he's. . .deserted. Deserted. That's what he's done. I've got no idea where you'd find him.'

'But you haven't deserted. You've just had a nervous breakdown.'

'I'm not well.' He lay back down on the bed. He certainly didn't look well. His eyes were so red you could have used them as tail-lights on a bike.

'So what happened that morning that made Julius desert and you collapse?'

'His friends came during the night and stole the corpse while we were asleep.'

'What?'

'You heard me. His friends came during the night and stole the corpse while we were asleep.'

'Do the temple authorities know this?'

'Yes. It was them who. . .Yes. They know.'

'When did you report this to the temple?'

'As soon as we could.'

'On that morning, April ninth?'

'Yes. As soon as we realised what had happened Corporal Publius and I ran to the temple and reported it.'

'Why didn't you go straight to the barracks and report it to your officers?'

'The sergeant had said we were assigned to the temple. He said the governor had agreed to provide them with a couple of guards, so we had to answer to them.'

Young Magnus was talking like a robot. His voice

was flat, and dull and lifeless. And what he was saying made no sense.

'So, what you're telling me is—'

'You heard me the first time. His friends came during the night and stole the corpse while we were asleep.'

I walked over to the window and flung back the shutters. Brilliant early morning sunlight streamed into the room. Magnus blinked and raised a hand to shade his face.

I sat down on his bed, and said, 'You're lying to me, young Magnus. You're lying to me and I don't like it.' I spoke quietly, but I could see the fear grip his face.

'No I'm not. I really—'

'Shut up and listen to me! If you fell asleep and let his disciples steal the corpse—then why aren't you dead?'

'But...I...'

'You know the rule in the Roman Army even better than I do. If a guard lets a prisoner escape, that guard has to serve the prisoner's sentence. And if the sentence is death, the guard is executed.'

'But he was already dead! We were only guarding a corpse!'

'The Roman Army doesn't run on kindness, young Magnus, so don't try to tell me it does. Guards who fall asleep on duty are punished. The discipline in the Roman Army is harsh. At the very least you would have been whipped and thrown into the guardhouse.'

'I...I...'

'You're lying, that's what you're doing! Show me your back!'

'Why? What's that got to do with...?'

I grabbed him, threw him against the wall, and pulled the shirt off his back.

'There's not a mark, young Magnus, not a mark. You haven't been whipped, you haven't been thrown into the guardhouse, you haven't been punished at all. Whatever happened that night, you didn't fall asleep, did you?'

'What happened—'

'DID YOU?' I bellowed.

'No,' he whimpered. 'No, we didn't fall asleep.'

I walked over to the window and looked out into the street for a minute to give the trembling young man a chance to pull himself together, then I turned around and bent over him. 'Do you know who hired me, young Magnus?'

'No, no I don't.'

'The temple authorities, that's who. And if you'd told them that his friends had come during the night and stolen the corpse while you were asleep, the temple bosses would never have hired me, would they?'

'I . . . I guess not.'

'Of course not! They would have picked up those "friends", thrown them into a cell, and beaten the new location of the corpse out of them. That's how they work, isn't it?'

'Yes, I guess . . .'

'Well, whatever you guess, young Magnus, that's what they would have done. They certainly would never have hired me. But they did—because they didn't know what happened, and they still don't. They haven't a clue. That's why they hired me. And that's what proves that your story is a load of old rope—a tissue of lies. Isn't it, young Magnus?'

'Yes, I guess—'

'So do I. I guess exactly the same as you. I guess that you know a lot more than you're telling. I guess that you saw something that night that made you collapse and your Corporal desert. And I guess you'd better start telling your Uncle Ben exactly what you saw, before your Uncle Ben beats the living daylights out of you.'

'Don't touch me! Don't touch me!' he almost shrieked.

Just then the door started to open. I didn't want bleeding-heart widow Goldblum fussing around, so I kicked the door closed and threw the bolt on the inside. She immediately began to pound on the door, yelling out, 'What are you doing to that boy in there?'

I ignored her, and sat down on the bed again.

'What I am doing in here,' I said very quietly to Magnus, 'is nothing compared to what I am going to do if I don't start getting some answers.'

'All right, all right,' he whimpered. 'I'll tell you what really happened.'

'Okay, that's better. Start at the beginning. When did you go on duty?'

'Just after sunset. The sergeant gave us a lantern, some hard-tack biscuits and a flask of brandy and told us to report to the temple for all-night guard duty.'

'And then?'

'Several of the priests told us what the job was, and they came down to the garden tomb with us. They properly checked that the slab was in place and the tomb was properly sealed, and stamped the wax seal with the chief priest's own mark, then told us to guard that tomb with our lives, and left us there.'

'You and Corporal Julius Publius?'

'Yes.'

'And then?'

'Well, we built a small fire to keep ourselves warm, and for most of the night we sat around the fire playing cards and talking—'

'Come on, get to the point!'

'I'm getting there. In the early hours of the morning, not long before dawn I would guess, but when it was still pitch black, there was an earthquake.'

'What earthquake?'

'Not a big one. But the ground shuddered and rumbled. And some loose rocks fell down from the top of the cliff. One of them thumped into the ground just a few feet away from us. So Publius decided to move further away.'

'And you didn't suggest to him that your duty was to stay near the tomb?'

'Huge lumps of rock had fallen down from the top of the cliff already. It wasn't safe. If there'd been another earthquake—'

'All right. So, what did you do?'

'We shifted to the other side of the garden, maybe a hundred yards away. I kicked some dirt over the fire, and we built a new one.'

Magnus Cassius shuddered involuntarily. 'It was kind of spooky.'

'Spooky?'

'Yeah, well, it was pitch black, and there was this earth tremble, and it was a dead man we were guarding after all. It sort of made the hairs stand up on the back of your neck. So Julius and I got stuck into the flask of brandy. To calm our nerves.'

'What happened then?'

'For a while, not much. But just at first light a woman arrived.'

'Who was it? Could you see her face?'

'Not clearly. She came through the gate and into the garden. She was some distance away from us. We could just see her through the trees.'

'Go on.'

'Well, she walked towards the tomb and, in no time—less than a minute—she came running back, in a sort of panic.'

'Where did she go?'

'Out of the garden, and back towards the city.'

'So what did you and Corporal Publius do?'

'We thought that, spooks or no spooks, we'd better take a look at the tomb. So, Julius drew his sword, and I carried the lantern, and we made our way through the garden to the entrance to the tomb.'

He stopped. There was a long silence, while his eyes grew vacant and his face filled with fear.

'Go on! You checked the tomb. And?'

'It was open.' He almost whispered it. 'The stone had been rolled back, and the tomb was open.'

'Who could have rolled back that stone?'

'How should I know?'

'The woman couldn't have done it.'

'No...I know, I know,' whimpered the young soldier.

'It takes two men to move those stones.'

'I know, I know. It couldn't have been the woman.'

'Then someone else must have come into the garden—and more than one.'

'Impossible. Julius or I would have heard them. There was no one else. The first person to come into that garden, after the priests left the night before, was the woman.'

'And you saw and heard nothing?'

'Nothing. We should have heard the stone being moved, but we didn't.'

'So what did you do next? Look inside?'

'Do you think we're mad? Of course, not! We don't go poking about inside tombs!'

'Okay. What did you do?'

'We ran to the temple, and reported to the priests. And they told us to say we had fallen asleep during the night and while we were asleep his friends had stolen the corpse. They said that they would put it right with the governor and make sure that we weren't punished.'

'And instead of being relieved, you were both so frightened that you collapsed and Corporal Publius deserted?'

'Yes. . .yes. . .yes. . .' he whispered. 'I've told you all I can. Now get out. Leave me alone.'

I left him lying on his bed, shivering. When I unbolted the door, and threw it open, Mrs Goldblum was standing on the landing, red-faced with anger.

'Make him some chicken soup, Mrs Goldblum,' I said. 'He needs it.'

Chapter 18

I walked back to the Landrover, convinced that Magnus Cassius had told me the truth, but not the whole truth. There was a gap in his story, somewhere, but, just for the moment, I had nothing to fill it with.

I drove across town to the office, honking my way through flocks of sheep and herds of goats, and carefully nudging my way around camels and donkeys. In Coppersmith Street I managed to find a small parking space that the chunky four-wheel drive would just squeeze into. Having parked and locked the vehicle I walked up to my office.

This time there were no nasty surprises—no waiting RIA men, and no mess of files all over the floor. I made myself some coffee, and began to worry that after cutting down on my alcohol I would get caffeine poisoning. Then I played back the messages on my answering machine.

Click.

'Benjamin, this is your Mama... You left home so early... Did you eat a proper breakfast? Are you coming home for lunch—a mother needs to know these things.'

Fast forward... Click.

'Bartholomew—this is Shagmar. I want a progress report. Ring me as soon as you come in.'

Click.

'BB, this is Sam. I forgot to tell you—the Landrover is low on juice, you'll have to fill it up. I know you, BB, you never check the fuel gauge. So, I thought I'd better remind you. Good luck with your case.'

Click.

That was all. I picked up the telephone and dialled.

'Shagmar—this is Ben Bartholomew.'

'You took your time. What progress can you report?'

'Well, you asked me to check on whether Jesus really died or not. I've spoken to the captain in charge of the execution squad, and the doctor who signed the death certificate. There's no doubt that when Davidson's body was taken down off the cross he was dead all right.'

'I see. Well, that was only ever an outside possibility, but it had to be checked. What about the Davidson crowd, where are they now?'

'As far as I can make out, they've all gone up to Galilee.'

'In that case, what are you doing in Jerusalem? Get after them!'

'Hold your horses, big boy. I'm off to Galilee first thing tomorrow morning. I've got just one more line to follow up before I go.'

'Who's that?'

'The lawyer, Nicodemus ben Gorion.'

'He's unimportant. Don't bother with him.'

'Look, if you want me to do this, let me do it my own way.'

'All right, but just don't waste time.'

'Don't worry. I'm right on top of it, big boy.'

'Have you had any more trouble from the RIA?'

'Have I what! They dragged me in to see Pilate last night.'

'Did they indeed? And what did he want?'

'He's just worried about stirring up local political hostility, that's all. He wants me to hose down any hotheads I run into, and hide anything I find that embarrasses him. He didn't quite put it like that, but that's what it adds up to.'

'Well, you just keep checking with me. I'll tell you what to tell the Romans and what not to tell them.'

'You're the boss.'

'That's right. And don't you forget it. Oh, and one other thing. . .'

'Yes, Chief?'

'That young guard, Magnus Cassius. . . Don't bother seeing him again, understand? He can't tell you anything of any use.'

'So you know I've been there?'

'I know a lot of things that go on in this city. So just don't bother young Cassius again. And keep in touch. Call me as soon as you get to Galilee.'

With a loud clunk the phone went dead.

Now that was interesting. Why did Shagmar want to stop me interrogating young Magnus? Did he know something the temple authorities wanted kept quiet? Or was Shagmar's reason even more devious? For the moment I had to leave the questions to rattle around in the back of my brain, in the hope that they would fall into place with the rest of the pieces and form a pattern.

I looked up Nicodemus ben Gorion's legal firm in the phone book, and called his secretary.

'Gorion, and Isaacson—can I help you?'

'I'd like an appointment to see Mr ben Gorion, please.'

'Hold the line a moment, sir.' I could hear the rustle of diary pages being turned over. 'How would next Wednesday morning be, sir?'

'It has to be today.'

'I'm afraid I don't think he can—'

'It's personal and it's urgent. His friend Joseph Arimathea put me on to him.'

'And your name is?'

'Bartholomew, Ben Bartholomew. I'm a private detective.'

'Just a moment, sir, I'll speak to Mr ben Gorion.' She came back less than a minute later. 'Mr ben Gorion can give you ten minutes at twelve-thirty today, sir. Will that be suitable?'

'I'll be there.'

That gave me some time to kill, so I did the part of the job I hate the most—the paperwork. I pulled out the Davidson file and started writing up the case notes. I suddenly realised, as I jotted down his story, what was screwy about what Magnus Cassius had told me. He said that when he and Corporal Julius Publius had gone back to the tomb they had found the stone rolled back and the tomb open. But they had not gone inside. I had specifically asked him that, and he had insisted that they had not gone in. Yet, when they had run to the temple and reported what they had seen the priests had immediately assumed that the body was missing. That's why the priests had given them that story to tell about friends coming in the night and taking the body.

But if all that the guards had seen was an open tomb, why did the priests assume the tomb to be empty and the body missing? Had young Magnus and his corporal actually seen more than just an open tomb? Had they, in fact, gone inside? Had they seen any other people in the garden that morning? There had to be more to the story than Magnus Cassius had so far told me, otherwise the priests would not have reacted the way they did. What else had Magnus seen? All questions with no answers—yet.

I finished writing up the case notes just as the big temple clock struck noon. I turned the answering machine on, and got my coat and keys. It was time to walk across town to Nicodemus ben Gorion's office.

Chapter 19

Just as I put my hand on the doorknob the phone rang and the answering machine started up. The volume was still turned up so I could hear what came next.

Click.

'You have called the office of Ben Bartholomew, Private Investigator. This office is temporarily unattended. Please leave your message after the beep.'

Beep.

'Mr Bartholomew...this is Magnus Cassius.' He was gabbling. 'I'll have to be quick. I'm in a public phone box. I'm sure Mrs Goldblum's phone is being tapped, and the house is being watched. I want to meet you. There's more... I'll come to your office tonight...late. Say, eleven o'clock. I've got the address.'

Click.

As soon as I knew who it was I'd run to grab the phone, but by the time I'd got there he'd hung up. Well, I would be sure to be in my office at eleven o'clock—that was one appointment I didn't want to miss.

Then I remembered the one with Nicodemus ben Gorion, and I hurried across town.

The lawyer's office was in a wedge-shaped building, a squat tower of glass and aluminium, in the heart of the business district. I checked the building directory and took the lift to the twelfth floor.

Opposite the lift I saw a brass plate which read:

BEN GORION, LEVI, SHAMIR & ISAACSON
Attornies at Law
Licenced Conveyancers
Sanhedrists

His secretary turned out to be one of those middle-aged women who mother their bosses. She would have made him lots of cups of tea and made him take his umbrella when he left the office. She probably reminded him of his wedding anniversary and his children's birthdays.

When I introduced myself she said, 'You're very punctual, Mr Bartholomew. Mr ben Gorion is waiting for you, come straight in.'

She led me down the corridor and ushered me into a large office that, very quietly and tastefully, smelt of money. The walls were lined with law books, and many of the pieces of furniture were valuable antiques.

The man himself rose from behind his leather-topped, rosewood desk and extended a hand in greeting. He had what is called, in polite circles, a 'tall forehead'. That is to say, his forehead continued as a shiny dome all the way to the back of his head. A fringe of dark hair ran from behind one ear, around to the back his head, to the other ear. This fringe seemed to continue in the form of a short, neatly trimmed beard that ran from in front of one ear, around a strong and resolute chin, to the other ear.

In the middle was a face that beamed cheerfulness and jollification. He looked more like every kid's favourite uncle than a heavyweight lawyer.

'I'm pleased to meet you, Mr Bartholomew,' he said as we shook hands, and so transparent was his sincerity that I think he really was glad to see me. 'Take a seat. Tell me what I can do you for.'

I showed him my licence.

'The corpse of Jesus the Nazarene has disappeared from its tomb,' I explained.

'I'm unsurprised, Mr Bartholomew, entirely unsurprised.'

'Oh, really? And why is that?'

'No tomb could ever have held him, Mr Bartholomew, no tomb. No tomb ever built, dug, or cut out of rock could ever have held the life that beats at the heart of the Cosmos. Jesus was…well…he was…the Mind of God, the Spirit of God, if you like, the Son of God. He was as much of God as could be fitted into one human body. Jesus was the Source.'

'The sauce?'

'The Source of all the life in the Universe. He was there in the beginning, Mr Bartholomew, in the very beginning to kick-start the Universe into life. You don't imagine any tomb could put an end to that, do you?'

'So you're telling me that he came back to life, rolled away the stone, and walked out of the tomb?'

'Well, either that, or else he walked through the molecules of the rock. After all, he made those molecules and they were under his command. Or else he matter-transmitted on a beam of pure energy out of the tomb. I don't know exactly how he did it, I only know that no tomb could ever have held him.'

'Are you serious, Mr ben Gorion?'

'Call me Nick, everyone does. And I'm deadly serious (although, in this case the adverb is inappropriate).'

'You're not joking? You're not taking the mickey out of me?'

'You'll know when I'm joking, Mr Bartholomew—you'll be laughing.'

Then he patted the shiny dome of his head. 'You see this?' he said. 'I always say that we men, when we're born, all have the same number of hormones. If you want to use yours to grow hair, that's your business,' and he laughed at his own joke. 'Anyway, they only put marble tops on quality furniture,' he added.

'And you're serious in what you say about the tomb?'

'Absolutely.'

'Now, you helped to lay him there.'

'That's right. My friend Joe and I did that.'

'On the Friday afternoon?'

'Yes, we had to hurry because it was late, and our law says that burials must be completed before the Sabbath begins at sunset.'

'Mr Arimathea obtained permission to take the body, and he brought the winding sheet and grave-clothes. What did you do?'

'I brought the spices, the myrrh and aloes, to be laid in the tomb with the body. And, of course, I helped Joe move the body, and lay it out in the tomb.'

Suddenly, all the jolliness left that grinning, cheerful face, and in a quiet serious voice he said, 'It was a sad, wasted, battered body. So beaten, so bruised, so cruelly treated.' And almost in a whisper he added, 'Never has a healthy young man been more cruelly beaten and killed, or so little deserved it.'

124

It was an embarrassing moment. I found it a little hard to know what to say. Having heard Lord Annas's reason for the execution, in my heart of hearts I agreed with him. What he, and Captain Longhinus, and Dr Theophilus, had told me about the crucifixion had horrified me. But I had an investigation to pursue. And if I didn't pursue it I would be beaten up by Shagmar. Maybe even killed.

'Did you know Jesus well?'

'Not well. But I did know him. I listened to him teach in public several times, and I went to him privately once to question him about his teaching.'

'What did you think of him?'

'Brilliant mind! Greatest intellect that ever lived!' he said with crisp certainty. Nicodemus's momentary melancholy was fading, and his constitutional cheerfulness was reasserting itself.

'I was in a meeting of the Sanhedrin once when a bunch of ding-a-lings wanted to arrest Jesus. I told them they were being outrageous, and managed to shut them up for the time being. But they turned out not to be ding-a-lings, but something rather nastier and grubbier.'

'What did they turn out to be?'

'Totally immoral and unprincipled conspirators!'

'Let's come back to that Friday afternoon at the tomb. You and Arimathea rolled the stone in place over the entrance, sealing the tomb?'

'That we did. When I woke up the next morning my arms and shoulders were aching, and it took several days for the grazes on my hands to heal.'

'So that stone is as hard to move as it looks?'

'Well, I wouldn't want to go ten-pin bowling with it, if you take my meaning.'

'What do you say about the theory that it was the

125

disciples of Jesus who came in the night and stole the body?'

'Nuts. That's what I say. That theory is just nuts. When Jesus was seized and executed the disciples fled in terror. They scattered, full of fears and tears. And you think they might have come back and stolen the body? Nuts! That's like suggesting that a bunch of rabbits turned up, overpowered the soldiers, and stole the body. Nuts!'

Just then the secretary stuck her head in the door. 'The conference in Mr Isaacson's office is just about to begin, Mr ben Gorion.'

'I'm just coming,' said Nicodemus. 'If you'll excuse me, Mr Bartholomew. I hope I have been of some help to you.'

Well, no, I thought, as I was going down in the lift, all you've done is to confuse me further.

Chapter 20

I walked slowly home, trying to figure out whether I had enough pieces yet to make the puzzle make sense.

In the kitchen I ate my way through one of Mama's big, hot lunches, in thoughtful silence.

'You're not talking to me, Benjamin. You sit down to lunch, and you're not talking to your Mama. What have I done to offend you this time?'

'You haven't done anything, Mama. I've just got a lot on my mind, that's all.'

'It's this case you're working on, isn't it? If it's worrying you that much, you should give it up. Listen to me. A mother knows.'

She didn't know how dangerous it would be for me to try to give up the case, and I didn't want to tell her. So I changed the subject.

'I saw Rachel yesterday, Mama.'

'You saw Rachel! I'm pleased, Benjamin. That warms a mother's heart. Where did you two meet? What did you do?'

'No, no, Mama. We didn't have a date. I just ran into her on the street, that's all.'

'I'm disappointed. First you build me up, then you let me down. Don't twist the knife, Benjamin. Mothers know they have to suffer for their children, it's the way God made us. So, anyway, you and Rachel just walked past each other and didn't speak, is that right?'

'No, we stopped and spoke. In fact, we sat down and had a cup of coffee together.'

'That's good, that's good. I like that. And how is Rachel looking?'

'She's looking fine, Mama. Just the way she always looked.'

'That pretty, huh? And is she happy?'

'I think so, Mama.'

'And is she married? That's the big question. Or engaged?'

'No, she's not married, or engaged.'

'There's still hope! Benjamin, there's still hope!'

Mama started to cluck and coo and I had to change the subject again. 'I have to pack my bags this afternoon.'

'Pack your bags? Where are you going?'

'Up to Galilee. Just for a few days.'

'So that's what you borrowed Mr Solomons' Landrover for. Now you drive carefully, Benjamin. You know what you're like on those long trips. You daydream and don't pay proper attention to the road.'

'I'll drive carefully, Mama.'

'And watch out for Zealots. They're out there in the hills, fighting those guerrilla battles with the Romans. Bullets flying everywhere! My God, my boy could be killed!'

'I'll be careful, Mama. I'll keep right away from the Zealots.'

That was one piece of Mama's advice I intended to follow. The last thing I needed at the moment was to get caught in a firefight between Zealots and Romans.

After lunch I packed a light travelling bag with some clean shirts, and some changes of underwear and socks. I cleaned and oiled my gun, reloaded it, and threw some extra ammunition in the bottom of the bag, underneath the socks.

Then, in the middle of the afternoon, my early start caught up with me, and I started to feel weary. So, I drew the curtains, lay down on the bed, and slept for an hour.

When I woke up I went to Coppersmith Street, and brought the Landrover back to my place. I parked right in front of the front door, and threw my travel bag in the back. I also loaded several canisters of fresh water, and made sure that the spare tyre and tool kit were intact.

After dinner I sat around reading the newspaper until ten-thirty. Then I put my gun into its shoulder holster, and set off for the office.

Coppersmith Street, late at night, was deserted, dark and chilly. The streetlights were pale, and only succeeded in making the shadows look darker and deeper. There was a chill wind blowing, like a river of air, like a ribbon of darkness, winding down the street. Halfway down the street, as I turned the corner into the alleyway, I heard a groan.

I pulled out my flashlight. On the ground near my feet was a thin trail of blood. I followed the trail with my light. It ended in a huddled body that lay at the foot of the stairs to my office. I turned and flashed the light around the rest of the alley. Deserted. There was another groan and I hurried back to the body.

It was Magnus Cassius. There was a bronze short sword buried to the hilt in his stomach. That made it a professional job. Amateurs always go for the head or the heart. But heads keep moving and are hard to hit, and hearts are smaller than most people think and are easy to miss. Professional hit-men always go for the stomach. They know that the victim will bleed to death.

I turned Magnus Cassius over onto his back. His eyes fluttered open and I turned the flashlight on my face, so that he could see who I was.

'Mr Bartholomew,' he wheezed. 'I was followed . . . Back at the corner he caught up with me . . .'

'Did you see who it was?'

He shook his head.

'Just lie still. I'll call the hospital.'

'No. There's no point. I've only got a few minutes. I'd rather die here than in an ambulance.'

He was right. Even if I got a doctor at once, nothing could be done. The young man was dying.

'Let me . . . tell you,' he gasped, each word coming out slowly and painfully, '. . . the rest of the story . . . the whole truth . . .'

And, leaving out the groans, and pauses, and gaspings for breath, this is what he told me:

'Have you ever seen an angel?' he asked.

'No,' I said, 'I've never seen an angel.'

'I have. That morning at the tomb, Publius and I saw an angel . . .'

'What did he look like?'

'. . . young man . . . dressed in white . . . during the earthquake . . .'

'Yes?'

130

'When the earth was trembling...Publius and I...we both saw him.'

'Where was he?'

'...right in front of the tomb. And he rolled away the stone... That's how the stone...the tomb was opened. He rolled it away... Just one hand...like it was a child's toy. And then—he sat on it. He rolled it away and sat on it.'

'And what did you and Publius do?'

'We were terrified. That's what really frightened us. Not the earthquake. It was...the angel...the huge stone that frightened us. You do believe it was an angel, don't you?'

'Sure, son, I believe you.'

'Publius and I...terrified. We shook with fear. We were like dead men. And we ran away...to hide...'

'Did you see anyone come out of the tomb?'

'No.'

'Did you see anyone else?'

'Later...the woman I told you... She was the first...in tears. A minute later...ran away...can't have been...more than a few seconds.'

'But there were others? Others you didn't tell me about before?'

'Yes... After the first woman...a group of women... They were there longer...Came back they were talking, laughing...happy.'

(Happy? People visiting a tomb were happy? This case just kept getting screwier all the time.)

Magnus's voice was getting fainter and he was finding it hard to talk.

'Then two men... They ran into the garden...out of breath... At the tomb for some time. And when they came back past where Publius and I were hiding they had their heads together, deep in conversation.

131

And then the first woman came back... I saw her...talking to the gardener... Then she left. No one else. When the garden was quiet...Publius and I crept out...reported what we had seen to the priests. And they said...they said...'

'Yes, I know what they said. With all this coming and going—could any of those people have been carrying a body when they left?'

'No. No one was carrying a body... Not the women... Not the two men... No one.'

'You absolutely sure?'

He tried to push himself up on one elbow, but failed. A trickle of blood ran out of his lips and down his chin.

'Yes,' he wheezed. 'Julius Publius, find him...he'll tell you...'

'Don't worry—I'll find him. You just lie back, son,' I said, not having a clue where I would start looking for a deserting Roman soldier.

'You do believe me, don't you?'

'Yes, of course I believe you, son. You just rest.'

A shudder passed through Magnus's body, and he groaned faintly.

I laid his head back gently, and went to find a phone box.

I called the police, anonymously, and told them where they could find the corpse of Magnus Cassius. It seemed I was spending a lot of my time in this case calling the police and telling them where to find corpses. All except for the corpse at the centre of the mystery. The one corpse I still couldn't find.

Chapter 21

The next morning before dawn, I was behind the wheel of the Landrover, heading out of town. As I kicked the engine into life I'd switched on the radio to get the news and weather forecast. The news bulletin contained my first bad news of the day. A Zealot guerrilla band had ambushed a Roman patrol on the Great North Road late the previous day. There had been a prolonged firefight, including shelling with mortars. The result was the Great North Road was closed to civilian traffic for some miles immediately to the north of Jerusalem.

When I heard that, I swung the wheel of the Landrover around. I had been planning to leave the city via the Sheep Gate and head directly north. I would now have to drive around the temple area, leave the city through the Horse Gate to the east, cross the Kidron Valley and take the Jericho road. That would take me more east than north, but I knew that somewhere past Bethany there was an unsealed back road that would take me back to the Great North Road.

It would add some hours to the journey, but I had no choice.

As I followed the road down into the Kidron Valley and up the other side I could see the Gihon Spring away to my right. The valley itself looked dry, and the vegetation brown. Soon I was back on the ridge, and heading for Bethany on the main Jericho road.

The countryside around me was rocky and sparse, and as the sun rose the day began to heat up. The Landrover ticked over like a dream, and I was grateful that those woad-painted Britons made such reliable vehicles.

As I drove, my mind was on what Magnus Cassius had told me the night before. The first question was: could he be trusted? He had lied to me twice before— once, when he repeated the story the priests had invented for him, and again when he had told me only part of the truth of what had happened that Sunday morning. On the other hand, the man was dying, and knew he was dying. Surely he wouldn't lie with his dying breath?

If he had told me the truth, that posed new problems. Suddenly the garden tomb had become as busy as Broadway on a Saturday night. Who were all these people? And what did all their comings and goings mean? It was clearly imperative that I identify all of them, and, if possible, question them all.

And there was at least one fact I knew that Magnus had got wrong. He claimed that he had seen the first woman, in the distance, talking to the gardener. Well, I knew that the gardener had been visiting his sister's family in Bethany that weekend. So, whoever that first woman had been talking to, it hadn't been the gardener. Who, then, could it have been? Or—another

134

question occurred to me—could the gardener have been lying?

On top of all this, I had promised Magnus that I would find his missing corporal, Julius Publius. Actually, I had promised that to keep a dying man happy, but the more I thought about it, the more tracking down Publius and grilling him thoroughly looked like a good idea. It seemed as if Ben was going to be one busy little detective for the next few days.

And then there was the argument, put up by Nicodemus, that, at the time, the friends of Jesus were as frightened as rabbits and it would have been psychologically impossible for them to steal the corpse. Well, Nicodemus was a lawyer, he was very intelligent, and he knew the people, so I couldn't discard his argument. But if he was right, that just re-opened the whole can of worms! How had the corpse vanished? And where was it now?

By the time I had sorted through these pieces of the puzzle, my head was spinning, I was past the Mount of Olives and about to enter the village of Bethany.

As I passed the outlying houses of the village I glanced at the fuel gauge. Empty! Then I remembered the message from Sam on the answering machine—I was supposed to fill the tank before I left Jerusalem!

Cursing myself for being all kinds of a fool, I pulled up in the quiet village street, turned off the engine, and got out to have a look around. It was a one-horse town, and it looked like the horse was still asleep.

There was only one street, with a few houses, a newsagent and general store, a post office, and a pub. And all was silence. No one was stirring. I walked slowly down the street, my joggers crunching softly in the dust.

Then, I thought I spotted some movement inside the post office. (Actually it was a post office at the front and a house at the back.) I went to the door and knocked.

Inside a woman's voice called: 'Abe, would you get the front door for me, please. Although who it can be at this time of the morning, I don't know.' Her voice trailed away. It sounded as though she were walking towards the back of the house.

Slipper-shod feet shuffled up to the other side of the door, bolts clanked and slid, and the door was flung open.

'What are you doing banging on doors at this time of the morn— Oh, it's you.'

The same words were going through my own head: 'Oh, it's you.'

The man who opened the door was the gardener from the garden tomb.

'So, this is your sister's house in Bethany?' I asked.

'Sure is. I notice you're not carrying your "authority" in your shoulder holster today.' (I was wearing a short-sleeved shirt for the hot drive.)

'That's right. But I've got it in the glovebox of the car. Do you want me to go and fetch it?'

'No, don't bother. You've got more questions I suppose?'

'Actually, all I wanted was to fill my tank with petrol.'

'Is that all? Well, that's easy. Just keep going the way you're facing. Another fifty yards down on your left, on your way out of town, there's a roadhouse with a petrol pump out the front. It used to be run by a man who died of leprosy five years back. Now it's run by his widow, and her sister, and their younger brother. They'll fill your tank.'

As he was talking his sister had shuffled up beside him. She was wearing a dressing gown and slippers, and had curlers in her hair. 'What does he want?'

'Only directions,' her brother replied, 'and I've given them to him.' He started to close the door, but I stuck out my foot and pushed it back.

'Mind if I ask you a question, ma'am?'

'What question?'

'Your brother here, did he stay with you over Passover?'

'Always does. Nothing different this year. Came on Friday, stayed for four days. That's right, isn't it, Abe?'

Abe just nodded, all he wanted was for me to go away.

'Thanks for your help,' I said, and turned to go. The door was slammed behind me and locks and bolts clicked and clanked into place.

I drove slowly up the street until, right on the eastern edge of the village, I came to a place with an old neon sign which said, 'Simon's Roadhouse'. I pulled up at the solitary petrol pump and tooted my horn.

Before the echo had died away a young man in blue overalls came sprinting around the side of the building. He grinned broadly, opened the driver's door for me, and said, 'Good morning, sir. What can I do for you?'

'Fill it up,' I said. 'Any possibility of breakfast, or is it too early?'

'No problem!'

And with that he ran—he didn't walk anywhere, this energetic young man, he ran—to the front door of the roadhouse and called out, 'Hey, Martha! Man here wants breakfast.' To me he said, 'If you'd care to take a seat inside, sir, you'll get breakfast in a jiffy.' Then he sprinted back to the pump.

Chapter 22

As I pushed open the swing door and walked into the little cafe, a homely looking woman with a cheerful round face called out from behind the counter, 'What would you like to eat?'

I looked at the blackboard menu, ordered an omelette and coffee, and sat down at a table near the front window.

For the next five minutes I watched in fascination as the bowser boy bustled around the Landrover. He pumped petrol; checked the water and oil; checked the air in all the tyres (including the spare); cleaned all the windows, front, side and rear; brushed the bodies of dead insects off the wire grill in front of the front windscreen; hosed the caked mud off the tyres and radiator. He didn't stop. It was hustle, and bustle and go, go, go. And the whole time he worked he smiled and whistled.

My observations were interrupted by the arrival of breakfast. It was served by an attractive, dark-haired woman. This, I thought, must be the younger sister.

'Is that your brother out there?' I asked, nodding towards the driveway.

'Yes,' she said. 'That's Lazarus.'

'Well, I'll tell you one thing for free—he's more full of life than any other young guy I've ever seen.'

She smiled, as if at some private joke, and said, 'Yes, you could put it like that.'

'I do put it like that! More full of life than any seven other people you could pick.'

With that I tucked into my breakfast. It was a light, fluffy omelette, full of herbs and garlic. I could feel it doing me good.

The waitress returned with a large mug of steaming hot coffee.

'Where are you heading for?' she asked, as she put the coffee on the table, 'if you don't mind me asking?'

'I don't mind. Ultimately, Galilee. But if I get as far as Sychar tonight I'll be happy. It all depends on how far I have to go out of my way to get around the Zealot roadblock.'

'You don't mind travelling through Samaria, then?'

'I'm not that sort of Jew.'

'Then what sort of Jew are you?'

'My mother is a Jew, so I'm a Jew. I eat the right foods, I go to temple occasionally—that sort of Jew.'

'I see. Well, there are only two types of travellers who use the Great North Road through Samaria— merchants and government officials.'

'Look, sister, do I look like a government official?'

'No, you don't. But then, you don't look like a merchant either.'

'That's very smart of you. What I am is a private investigator.'

'A detective?'

'A private detective.'

139

'And what, exactly, are you detecting?'

'I'm tracking down a bunch of religious fanatics who belong to a group called the Jesus Movement.'

With that her face went pale, and the light that had been sparkling in her eyes went dim.

'You know them, don't you?' I challenged.

'Are they in trouble?'

'Not with me, they're not.'

'Then with the people who hired you?'

'Possibly. They've stolen something, and my employers want it returned.'

At this, she looked puzzled. 'But they wouldn't steal anything,' she said. 'I know them. I know them well. They are plain, honest people.'

'Well, if they didn't steal anything, then they won't be in trouble.'

She still looked worried. And it occurred to me that she might be able to give me some useful information. 'Look, if they really are the plain, honest people you say they are, I can help them.

'My employers are very powerful,' I said. 'What happens to your friends depends on my report. If I can find them quickly, if I can talk to the ones who are really in charge, and if I can send back a report that clears them—well, there won't be any trouble, see?'

'I see. And I can see that you would like me to help you.'

'Just an address, that's all, sister. I know they've gone to Galilee, but I don't know where in Galilee. Help me get to the right people, and maybe I can save them a lot of trouble.'

'How do I know I can trust you?'

'Look at my honest face.'

She did. She stared at me intently for a full minute. It was most disconcerting.

140

'Look,' I said, 'I've got no axe to grind with these friends of yours. My assignment is to recover something that's been stolen, that's all. If you trust your friends, if you know they are honest people, tell me where to find them. I can clear them of suspicion, and save them a lot of trouble.'

'They are plain, honest people,' she repeated, 'and I do trust them. All right then, I'll tell you. Once you meet them, talk to them, I know you'll be impressed by them, and you won't want to cause them any trouble.'

'Where do I find them, then, in Galilee?'

'I don't know where they are precisely, right at this moment, but I suggest you try Bethsaida.'

'Bethsaida?'

'On the north-eastern shore of the lake.'

'I know where it is. And who should I speak to?'

'Any one of the Eleven. Peter is taking the lead in most things, but any one of the Eleven will be able to help you.'

'The Eleven? They sort of the board of directors, are they?'

'Yes. Talk to them.'

Just then the older sister's voice rang out from the kitchen, 'Mary! I've been washing up for ten minutes, come and start drying.'

'I'll have to go,' said Mary. 'I'm always talking when I should be working,' and she hurried away.

I finished my coffee in a leisurely fashion, left enough money on the table to cover the bill—with a tip for the information I had collected—and walked out to the driveway.

By this time, Lazarus was polishing up the battered and scratched duco of the vehicle. Sam's old Landrover had never looked so good.

'What do I owe you?' I asked.

He named the price of the petrol. The rest of the service, it seemed, was free. I paid him, gave him a tip, climbed into the Landrover and started off.

I drove out of Bethany congratulating myself on my brilliant strategy of calling into the village. That little town had turned out to be a goldmine of information.

I had been able to confirm that the gardener was visiting his sister over the Passover weekend, so whoever young Magnus had seen the woman talking to in the garden that Sunday morning, it wasn't the gardener.

And I now had a destination in Galilee to head for. That information could cut my investigation time in half. I was so busy congratulating myself, that I almost missed my turn-off.

Chiselled into the face of a flat, roadside milestone, in neat Roman lettering, were the words:

TO GREAT NORTH ROAD
SAMARIA
GALILEE

and underneath was an arrow. That's another good thing about the Romans—their signposting. Very thorough about it they are, as a rule. Mind you, in my part of the world, Zealots are always coming along and pulling down the signposts, so, in the end it doesn't do much good. I swung the Landrover onto the road.

It was not one of your classic Roman roads.

For a start, it had been laid out by a drunken surveyor (possibly on a pitch-black night), and, as a result, it did not seem to be in any particular hurry to get anywhere. It took the scenic route. It ambled and meandered across the countryside (Amble and Meander sound like a firm of cheap divorce lawyers) paying homage to every little hillock and dip and, like a drunk taking giant steps over tiny obstacles, the road gave wide and cautious berth to even the smallest hill.

It had also been carefully designed to be exactly eighty per cent as wide as the average motor vehicle, with the result that one pair of wheels had, at all times, to be travelling in ruts and ditches.

I had to slow right down, and engage the four-wheel drive as the corrugations on the unsealed surface started to undulate like waves on a beach.

'This is ridiculous,' I thought. 'I'm starting to feel seasick—and I'm thirty miles from the coast.'

About the middle of the morning I stopped under the shade of a spreading fig tree. I got out and walked around to stretch my legs. Then I went to the water canister, had a drink, and splashed water over my face and hands.

After a twenty-minute break I got back into the vehicle determined not to stop again until I reached the main road. It was a decision I was to regret many times, over the next six hours, as the dusty road twisted and corrugated, as the Landrover shook and rattled, and as the muscles in my arms ached from wrestling with the steering wheel.

But every battle ends sooner or later, even battles with bucolic backroads, and, about the middle of the afternoon, I turned onto the main road heading north. I parked in the first shade I came to and got out to walk around and stretch.

My shirt was soaked with sweat, my behind was sore, all my muscles were stiff. I washed and drank again, and dug a couple of apples out of the bag of fruit my mother had packed me.

After maybe a quarter of an hour I climbed reluctantly back into the vehicle to continue my journey.

The Great North Road was straight, flat, and smooth: Roman civil engineering at its most civil. I was able to push Sam's old Landrover along a good bit quicker, and that, in turn, pushed a cooling breeze through the vehicle.

Despite the good road, it was almost sunset before I hit the town of Sychar. Facing the central square of the town was the flashing neon sign of 'The Wellview Motel' with the welcoming addition: 'Vacancies'. I gratefully pulled into its courtyard, and staggered wearily to the reception desk.

Chapter 23

I showed the reception clerk my driver's licence, and signed the register. She handed me a key and said (in the flat, nasal voice that seems to be compulsory for all reception clerks), 'Room seven, up the first flight of stairs'.

A hot, soaking shower repaired the damage of the day. With the dust and grime washed away, and my aching muscles eased by the jets of hot water, I felt ready to eat.

It was late when I went downstairs, and the dining room was almost deserted. In a corner an elderly couple were lingering over coffee, and a young couple with two small children were just leaving.

I had ordered a tuna salad, and was sipping a glass of iced water when a chubby little bald guy, with a drooping moustache and far too much energy for a hot, humid evening, bustled into the dining room.

As he glanced around the room I thought to myself, 'Not my table, don't invite yourself over here,

I'm too tired.' Of course, Bartholomew's Law of Opposites went to work at once—he headed straight for my table.

'Mind if I join you?' he asked.

I was too tired to reply, and he pulled out a chair and sat down.

'I'm late for dinner,' he explained. 'Just tying up a big order with a local builder. The name is Cleopas,' and he stuck out his chubby little fist.

'Ben,' I said, shaking the offered hand.

He called over the waitress, ordered pasta and beer, and started babbling in a loud, hearty voice.

'I'm a traveller,' he said. 'Building materials, mainly terracotta. Whatever you want in terracotta I can supply—roofing tiles, floor tiles, large water jars, fancy decorations—we make the lot. Emmaus Terracotta Incorporated—that's us. My brother runs the factory, I do the selling. Give me a call if you ever need any terracotta.' He thrust his card at me.

'And what do you do yourself?' he asked. 'What's your line?'

'Crime,' I muttered, not feeling talkative.

His eyebrows shot up so high there was a momentary risk they would become completely detached. 'You a cop?'

'Private detective.'

'Hey, that must be exciting work! Are you on a case now?'

'Yep.'

'What is it? Murder?'

'The cops chase the murderers.'

'Don't tell me you're chasing a naughty husband.' He sounded disappointed.

'I don't do divorce work.'

'Then what's your special patch?'

146

'Missing persons. Recovering stolen property. That sort of thing.'

'What case are you on now?' he leaned forward and whispered mysteriously. 'If you're allowed to tell me, that is.'

'Stolen property.'

'Something important?'

'I'm told it is.'

'Valuable?'

'Hard to say.'

'What is it? Come on. You can tell me.'

I was too tired to resist him. 'A corpse,' I explained.

'A corpse? Hey that sounds interesting! Whose corpse?'

'Jesus the Nazarene.'

His expression changed. His face closed up. From being wide-eyed and fascinated it became as blank as a pudding.

'What do you know about Jesus?' he asked, suddenly subdued.

'Only what I've been told: that he was executed by the Romans, at the request of the temple authorities, on the Friday of Passover week, and that thirty-six hours later his corpse was missing from the tomb where it had been sealed behind a stone slab.'

'Is that all you've heard?'

'I've heard a lot of details, but in the end they don't add up to much more than that.'

'I can tell you more,' he said in an excited voice. He was one of those people who couldn't remain subdued for long. His face had lit up again, not with curiosity this time, but with the expression of a child with a story to tell.

'Tell me.'

'I've seen him.'

'Jesus?'

'Yeah, Jesus.'

'Well, so what? Lots of people saw him. He was a public figure.'

'No, no, no! I've seen him *since*.'

'Since when?'

'Since the execution, dummy.'

'You're not making any sense. Exactly when did you see him?'

'On the day the corpse vanished. On the Sunday.'

I looked at him hard. He didn't look loopy. He looked normal. Well, as much as a travelling salesman is ever normal.

'You saw him on the Sunday after he was executed?'

'That's what I'm telling you!'

'Where?'

'On the bus to Emmaus.'

'Tell me about it.'

'My brother and I were going home after Passover. We were part of his group, you know, we were disciples. And we were sitting there feeling shattered, just destroyed. We had thought that Jesus had brought in a whole New Age, a New Hope. He had come to rescue the world. But with the execution, it had all ended. Our hopes had died.'

The tuna salad and the pasta were delivered to our table, but that didn't stop the little salesman's flow of words.

'My brother and I,' he said, 'were sitting there talking about it all, our hearts pretty much in our boots, when this guy came and sat down beside us at the back of the bus. "What are you talking about?" he said. "What do you think we're talking about?" I said. "What all Jerusalem is talking about," I said. "And what's that?" he said. "Where have you been?"

I said. "Have you been in solitary confinement?" I said. "Don't you ever look at newspapers?" I said. "Jesus of Nazareth," my brother explained. "The chief priests wanted him killed, so the Romans killed him. And this morning when the women in our group went to his tomb it was empty. And they said they spoke to an angel who told them he is alive.'' "And then some of the others went to the tomb," I said. "And they came back saying they had found it empty," I said. And when I had finished, this guy started explaining things. Just like a rabbi in Sabbath school when I was a kid, he quoted the scriptures and explained what they meant. He went through it bit by bit. Moses and the prophets and everything. All about how human beings could only be rescued by a God who would come into this world and suffer on their behalf. It was fascinating stuff.'

Cleopas stopped to mop his chubby face with a big, white handkerchief. Then he continued, 'Well, when the bus got to Emmaus my brother and I said, "Come and have lunch", and this guy said "Okay". And when we sat down to lunch we asked him to say grace, and when he was saying grace we suddenly realised who he was: it was Jesus!'

'You didn't recognise him before that?'

'No, no, we just didn't recognise him.'

'Why not? Did he look different?'

'Not different. No, definitely not different?'

'Then why didn't you recognise him?'

'My brother and I talked about that. We reckon it was because we didn't *expect* to see him. We thought he was dead. We believed that. And I guess we didn't take too close a look at the guy on the bus. And because our hearts didn't believe, they wouldn't let our eyes see who it really was. But when he said grace

149

at our table, it was just so familiar, the way that he did it, that it hit us like a ton of terracotta—it was him!'

'Not a ghost?'

'Do I look loopy? Of course not a ghost! I don't believe in ghosts.'

'But you do have conversations with dead men?'

'I know it sounds screwy, but I tell you it happened. I've only ever spoken to one dead man in my life, and that was Jesus. And that was a special case because Jesus is a special case. He is the God who came to suffer for us, and rescue us. And conquering death is just part of that. If you see what I mean?'

'I see what you mean,' I lied.

'I knew you would,' he said. 'That's why I told you about it. You were real friendly to me when I came in to dinner tonight. You're a nice guy. So, I wanted to tell you.'

'About the bus to Emmaus?'

'Specifically, I wanted to tell you that you're wasting your time. If you've been hired to find the corpse of Jesus of Nazareth, you're never going to be able to deliver on that contract.'

'Because there is no corpse?'

'Because there is no corpse. Jesus is alive again. I've met him. I've seen him. I've talked to him. There is no corpse for you to find.'

This guy was loopy, I decided. He didn't look loopy, but looks can deceive. Yes, I thought, definitely loopy.

'Aren't you worried,' I asked, 'what the temple authorities might say, if you go around spreading a story like that?'

'The temple authorities can go jump! I'll tell anyone I feel like telling, and they won't stop me!'

Definitely loopy, I thought, definitely loopy. 'I'm

whacked. It's been a long day, and I've got to crawl into bed before I collapse on the spot.'

He was a sincere little guy, and he didn't spot my escape excuse.

'But thanks for what you told me,' I said. 'You've helped me a lot.'

He beamed. 'I'm glad. You look like a nice guy, so I didn't want you to waste your time looking for something that's not there.'

'Yeah, well that's real nice of you,' I said, as I backed towards the door. 'Thanks for your help.' And I turned and escaped to my room.

Chapter 24

That night I slept badly. After my exhausting day I should have toddled off to dreamland like a baby. But I didn't. I tossed and turned all night. By dawn I was so wide awake I got out of bed and put on the jug to make myself a cup of coffee. I realised that it was the loopy little terracotta salesman who had rattled me so much that I couldn't sleep.

Then it hit me, like a ton of Cleopas's terracotta. It was vital that I talk to that guy again. Loopy or not, that terracotta traveller had information I needed.

This Cleopas called himself a disciple, he had been in Jerusalem that Sunday, and he might be able to fill in some blanks for me. I was trying to sort out that list of comings and goings in the garden that Magnus Cassius had told me about and Cleopas could put names to some of those people.

I dressed hastily, and hurried down to reception. The same nasal voiced clerk was back on duty.

'There's a guy staying here,' I said, 'a terracotta

salesman, Cleopas something—I don't know his last name. Do you know the man I mean?'

'Yes, sir.'

'I want to catch him before he checks out. He hasn't gone yet, has he?'

'No, sir, not yet. He left a call for an eight o'clock breakfast. I would suggest, sir, that you wait until after eight before you disturb him.'

'Sure, sure. And his room?'

'Number eight, sir. He's your neighbour.'

I thanked her and went back to my room, showered, shaved, and dressed again, at a more relaxed pace. My own breakfast arrived at seven-thirty. I made sure I had finished my breakfast, and coffee, and cleaned my teeth, by eight o'clock.

At eight I heard the breakfast tray being delivered to Cleopas next door. Giving him fifteen minutes to eat, I re-packed my light travel bag, took the bag downstairs and locked it in the back of the Landrover. Then I paid my bill, and went back upstairs to room eight.

My knock was greeted by a cheerful, 'Come in.'

Cleopas was already dressed and packed and ready to leave. 'Oh, it's you, Ben. How are you this morning? Sleep well? You looked really tired last night.'

'Yeah. I'm fine, thanks. Look, you've already helped me a lot with information, can you help me again?'

'Why not? Nothing I know is a secret.'

'Go back in your mind to that Sunday.'

'The Sunday I saw Jesus on the bus to Emmaus?'

'That's right. I gathered that you and your brother were with his friends when the women came back and reported the tomb empty?'

'That's right. We were together that morning. Misery loves company.'

153

'Tell me what happened.'

'What happened in the afternoon was more important—when I found out for sure that Jesus had come back.'

'Yes, I can see that. But I need to understand what happened in the morning, if you don't mind.'

'I don't mind. If it's really important to you, I'll try to remember.'

'Okay. Start with where you were staying, and who was there.'

'Well, the disciples had a sort of a base in Jerusalem. It's a house owned by a wealthy widow named Mary. Incidentally, there are about half a dozen different women I know named "Mary", so I hope this doesn't get confusing. Anyway, this particular Mary is, as I say, a wealthy widow. She has a teenage son—boy named John Mark, nice kid. And she has a big house with a lot of spare rooms so Jesus and his friends used it as a sort of base when they were in Jerusalem.'

He mentioned the address. It was the place I had gone to and found empty when I was first looking for Mary Magdalene.

'This wealthy widow,' I said, 'her surname's not "Magdalene" is it?'

'No, that's another Mary. I told you it might get confusing. Anyway, staying at this house during Passover was the mother of Jesus—her name's Mary too, so I hope you're keeping track of this. In fact, there were four Marys in the house: Mary the mother of Jesus, Mary Magdalene, another Mary married to a man named Clopas with a son named James, and the Mary who owned the house (the widow). Are you following this?'

'I haven't lost the plot so far.'

'As well as the four Marys there was Salome (the sister of Mary the mother of Jesus—in other words, Jesus' aunt) and Joanna. Now Joanna's husband is Chuza, and he's got a big job in Herod's palace—one of the stewards, or something like that. So Joanna usually sleeps at the servants apartments at the palace with her husband, but that weekend she stayed at the house just to be close to the others—everyone being so upset.'

'That's the women, what about the men?'

'Not much actually. In fact, there were only two: Peter and John. The others had all taken off for the hills when Jesus was arrested. I think they spent the weekend in Bethany, with a couple of sisters who own a roadhouse there.'

'I've met them.'

'Right. Well, most of the guys spent the weekend there, and only Peter and John were in Jerusalem. Oh, and the teenager, John Mark.'

'What about you and your brother, weren't you there?'

'No, I've got my own apartment in the city—because I have to go there so much on business, you see. So my brother and I stayed in the apartment, and we went across to see the others at the house after breakfast.'

'Now, last night you mentioned that some women had gone to the tomb very early. . .'

'And found it empty.'

'And found it empty. Precisely. But, which women? Who went?'

'Well. . . As I understand it, the arrangement was that Mary Magdalene and the other Mary—married to Clopas, son named James—and Salome and Joanna were all going to go together. Mary Magdalene had organised it all on the Saturday night—she was a bit of a leader and organiser amongst the women. But it didn't quite work out like that.'

'What did actually happen?'

'Well, as she explained it to us later, it turned out that Mary Magdalene couldn't sleep. She just lay in bed tossing and turning half the night. Finally, she couldn't stand it any longer and she got up and, even though it wasn't even dawn yet, she decided to go to the tomb ahead of the others. If you ask me, she was so upset she wanted to have some private crying time at the tomb. Anyway, she left a note for the other women saying she had gone on ahead, and she walked to the tomb. But when she got there she found it standing open, the big stone rolled away. Well, she just took it for granted that the body had been stolen, and ran back to the house at top speed. She woke up Peter and John and told them what she had found, and all three of them ran back to the tomb. But in the meantime, while Mary was away, the other women had woken up, had found her note, and had set off for the tomb too.'

'Which other women?'

'The three I mentioned—the other Mary (wife of Clopas, mother of James), Salome and Joanna. Well, you know what the streets are like in that part of the city—a mass of twisting, interconnecting lanes, with half a dozen narrow streets all leading in much the same direction. Because of that these three women missed Mary running back. In fact, they must have missed her twice.'

'Twice?'

'You'll understand in a minute. While Mary Magdalene was running back, these three women were arriving at the tomb, but, unlike Mary, when they found it open they went inside—and saw an angel. Have you ever seen an angel?'

I remembered that Magnus Cassius had asked me the same question.

'No,' I said.

'Neither have I. But these three say there was an angel sitting in the empty tomb. He told them—are angels "he"?'

'I don't know.'

'Neither do I. Anyway, this angel said that Jesus had risen from the dead, and that he would meet them in Galilee—'

'That's why so many of the group have gone to Galilee?'

'Now you're catching on! The Eleven have gone to Galilee, and a lot of the others too. I'm heading up that way myself as soon as I've finished here.'

'What else did this angel say?'

'That the women were to go back to the disciples and report what they had seen and heard. So, the three women headed back to the house. On the way out of the garden they saw Jesus himself. He stood there in front of them for a moment and told them he would be waiting for them in Galilee. Well, you can imagine the excitement! Or, then again, maybe you can't. All of this is a unique experience—never happened in the world before, will never happen again.'

'Keep going. What happened next?'

'Well the three women hurried back to the house. And this was the second time they missed Mary Magdalene. I guess it all depends on which of those narrow twisting streets you choose to take.'

'And while the women were doing this, what was happening to Mary Magdalene and the two men she had woken up—Peter and John, wasn't it?'

'That's right. Well, all three of them ran to the garden tomb. John got there first, found the tomb open, but waited for the others. Peter arrived next and he rushed straight into the open tomb. That's Peter all over—always impetuous. They saw that the body was missing, but the graveclothes were lying there undisturbed, and they walked back slowly to the house, puzzled and disturbed. Last of all Mary Magdalene arrived back at the garden (Peter and John had run on ahead of her—and she had been too puffed to keep up). So, there she was in the garden, by herself, in tears... And Jesus was there, and he spoke to her.'

'What did he say?'

'He comforted her. And gave her the same message: he would meet everyone in Galilee.'

'So Mary—Mary Magdalene, that is—and three other women had seen Jesus, and I guess everyone was pretty excited when they came back to the house and reported?'

'Well... if I was to be entirely honest with you, Ben, I would have to admit that we didn't believe them. Not even Peter and John—I mean, they were only women, weren't they?'

'Well, it is pretty hard to believe.'

'Exactly—I knew you'd understand. But then that afternoon Jesus appeared to my brother and me on the bus to Emmaus, and we hurried back to Jerusalem. And that night, the Sunday, Jesus suddenly appeared at the house when we were all together— well almost all of us—and then everyone believed.'

It was clear that chubby little Cleopas believed. His sincerity was transparent. But did I believe? No. That's the honest answer. Mind you, it did fit exactly the story that the Roman soldier, Magnus Cassius, had told me—and that shook me a bit.

I thanked Cleopas for his help, shook his hand, and said goodbye. It was time to get going again: heading north on the next stage of my journey.

I hurried out to the Landrover in the courtyard of the motel, kicked it into life, and pulled out onto the main road.

Chapter 25

The Great North Road lay before me—straight and true as a sword fresh from the bronze-smith. The Landrover ate up the ribbon of road like a spring-loaded tape measure when you press the re-wind button. The day was only starting to warm up, and there was a cool breeze blowing through the car. Over the smooth surface the tyres hummed like a barber shop quartet singing close harmony on a Saturday night.

As I drove, I thought.

Had I learned anything useful from the little terracotta salesman? Well, yes I had. He had fed me his friends' standard account of what happened to the body of Jesus the Nazarene. It was useful to know that. In whatever way the corpse had come to vanish, it was clear that Jesus' friends believed the story that Cleopas had told me. Which made it sort of difficult for them to be the body-snatchers. But, would I discover more devious and manipulative people when I met the Eleven? I would find the answer to that question in Bethsaida.

The most useful thing that Cleopas had done for me was to attach names to the people who visited the garden tomb that Sunday morning. I now knew that I needed to track down Mary Magdalene, the other Mary (wife of Clopas, mother of James), Salome, Joanna, Peter and John. Six people. A tall order. In reality, if I could just nail down two or three of them that would help.

The day became a baker's oven, and I became a loaf of bread. I had one of the water canisters on the seat beside me, and every half hour or so I had a drink, and splashed my face. The Great North Road, like so many great highways, bypasses the small towns, which relieved me of the temptation to stop, and so I barrelled on through the morning.

At about lunchtime, I hit the major T-intersection where the Great North Road meets the coast road. A left-hand turn would take me towards Caesarea and the sea, while a right-hand turn would take me to Tiberias on the shores of Lake Galilee. I turned right.

Perhaps an hour later I was on the outskirts of a small town. The signpost said 'Nazareth'. That gave me two good reasons to stop. The first was to fill up with petrol, and get something to eat, and the second was the possibility that in the home town of Jesus Davidson I might learn something useful.

The main township was south of the highway, so I turned off the coast road towards the small cluster of buildings and I pulled into the town's only petrol station, and, as the tank was being filled asked the attendant, 'Is there anywhere I could get something to eat around here?'

'That white building just down a ways,' he said, indicating the direction with a nod of his head. 'That's the pub. You might try there.'

'I might leave the Landrover here, and walk over, if you don't mind?'

'Take as long as you like, it don't bother me.'

I walked down the street towards the white building. It was just after lunchtime, that still, hot hour in the early afternoon, when the whole world seems to sleep. I could smell the eucalyptus trees, hot and sharp in the still air. An old, brown dog was lying in the shade, asleep. He didn't even bother to lift his head as I passed.

There was a sign across the front of the building, a sign that still whispered through its faded, peeling paint, 'Nazareth Hotel'. I stepped into the bar, and plunged out of the glare of the street into gloom. Slowly my pupils adjusted and the scene swam into focus. Except for two customers playing cards in a corner, the place was empty.

Behind the counter the barman was smoking and reading a magazine. I ordered a beer. He took my money and served the drink without saying a word. He was about to go back to his magazine, when I asked, 'Got anything to eat?'

'You're too late. Counter lunches are off.' It was hard to tell whether he meant forever, or just for the day. Then he took pity on me. 'But I can get you a sandwich if you like. Cheese and pickle?'

'That'll do fine.'

He disappeared out the back, and returned a moment later with a sandwich that appeared to have been left over from yesterday's counter lunch, or possibly last week's. I was very hungry, so I tried very hard not to think about it while eating the sandwich. At least the beer was cold and washed away the taste.

'Bartender.'

'Yeah?'

'Do any of the Davidson family still live in town?'

'Didn't you notice?'

'Notice what?'

'The timberyard opposite. . .'

I walked to the door of the bar and looked out. On the opposite side of the street was a sign reading 'Davidson Timber Incorporated'. I turned to thank the barman, but he had gone back to his magazine and cigarette. I strolled across the street and through open double gates into the timberyard. Towards the front of the yard was a small office. Squeezed behind a small desk, and drowning in files and letters, was a secretary pounding away at an ancient manual typewriter. She ignored my entrance and kept on typing.

'Excuse me,' I said, and the clatter stopped.

'Yes?'

'Are any members of the Davidson family in today?'

She called out, 'Jim! Man to see you!' and went back to her typing.

A man stepped out of the inner office. Tall, dark hair, brown eyes. He slightly resembled the man in the photograph Shagmar had given me—but younger.

'Come in,' he said, and waved me to a larger office with a slowly revolving ceiling fan.

I sat down in a battered old green chair. He perched on the edge of the desk.

'What can I do for you?'

I showed him my licence. He looked at it without interest, and repeated, 'What can I do for you?'

'It's about your brother,' I said, taking a guess, 'your older brother.'

'What about him?'

'I don't know if anyone has broken the news to you, but your brother's body has been stolen from his tomb in Jerusalem.'

163

'Not "stolen". The body is missing from the tomb, but it hasn't been stolen.'

'Then you do know something about it?'

'Yes—yes, I do.'

'Why do you say "missing" but not "stolen"?'

'Because you can't steal something that belongs to you.'

'Are you telling me that you, as the brother of Jesus, went and took the body?'

With that his solid face lost its wooden expression, and broke into a broad grin. 'Of course not!'

'What then?'

'His body doesn't belong to me, or to any other member of his earthly family. It belongs to him—and he took it.'

'It was Jesus who removed his own body from the tomb?'

'Surely you have spoken to some of the disciples? They will have told you.'

Then the drachma dropped. This man was a 'disciple' himself. He believed the same story that Cleopas had told me.

'I guess I shouldn't be surprised to find that you are a disciple yourself,' I said.

'Well, you should be. Everyone here in Nazareth is. During his lifetime I didn't understand who Jesus really was...or is, rather...and what his mission was.'

'But now you do understand? And believe? What changed your mind?'

'He came to me. Not long after he had risen from his tomb, he visited me, spoke to me. The Jesus who had conquered death opened my eyes to what I had failed to see in the purely earthly Jesus. He was my brother, and is still that, but his family is bigger now,

164

and he is brother to any who will take his name. On top of which, he is more than brother to me now, he is my Master.'

I was wasting my time. It was like talking to Cleopas all over again.

'I've got to be going,' I said. 'Thanks for your time.'

'You wanted to ask me something.'

'I've changed my mind. I don't think you can help me. Thanks for your time.'

He held out his hand, and I shook it—a rough, calloused, timber worker's hand.

I hurried out of the office, out of the timberyard, and back to my vehicle. The attendant had moved it into the shade of a sycamore tree, which was thoughtful of him. I paid for my petrol, got into the Landrover, and drove back onto the main road.

Within minutes I was heading east, barrelling down the highway towards Tiberias and Lake Galilee.

Chapter 26

Before long the road came to the edge of the escarpment, and began winding down the steep, rocky slope into the Jordan Valley. Suddenly, a thousand feet below, there was a strip of bright blue—Lake Galilee.

As I drove steadily downhill into the trench of the valley, the air grew hotter. Soon I could make out the patch of green palm trees and oleanders and then the white roofs of Tiberias, hundreds of flat-roofed, white houses marching down a gentle hill slope, to the lakeside. Dominating the whole scene were the soaring Roman pillars of Herod's palace.

My plan was to continue north around the side of the lake, and spend the night at one of the lakeside towns—possibly Magdala. Tiberias, Herod's new capital (named in grovelling honour of the Emperor in Rome), was a largely Gentile city, and, I thought, of little use in my investigation.

But then the weather blew in and changed my mind. One moment the sky was clear and the air oven-hot, the next a wind began to rush down on the lake out of the west, bringing with it a steadily mounting bank of black clouds. In half an hour the clouds were filling the sky from horizon to horizon, with a rolling, threatening, black blanket. Then came the first flashes of lightning and the first peels of thunder. By the time I had reached the foothills the rain had started.

The temperature dropped rapidly, and I had to pull over to the side of the road to get a jacket out of my bag. With the jacket to keep me warm I continued the journey, driving slowly and carefully into the teeth of pelting, thundering, wind-driven rain. The roof of the Landrover started to leak, and the windscreen wipers worked only intermittently. As I drove I cursed the woad-painted makers of the vehicle. You would expect that the inhabitants of that rain infested island would at least design a vehicle for wet weather use!

But then, it was a very old Landrover that had seen long and faithful service. When I got back to Jerusalem I would give Sam a swift kick for not maintaining it properly.

The rain became heavier, and the visibility worse. I was crawling along, anxiously scanning the road for each twist and turn. I couldn't drive much further through this torrential rain. So I made up my mind to spend the night in Tiberias, and continue my journey in the morning.

When I reached the outskirts of the city, still crawling and nursing my vehicle, the streets were deserted, and the gutters overflowing.

Have you ever tried to pick your way through the streets of a strange city in a thunder storm? I don't recommend it. Even the street signs were impossible to read. After a while I realised that the white-walled buildings were only on one side of the car. I had driven right through the town and come to the edge of the lake. Ahead of me was a long timber wharf that ran out into the boiling, stormy water. In the flashes of lightning I could see, tied up at various points along its length, fishing boats bouncing in the wind-driven waves.

With one hand shielding my eyes from the rain, and the other holding the flashlight, I staggered to the other side of the street. As I approached the building facing the wharf I could dimly make out a lighted window. My flashlight picked out a sign swinging crazily in the wind: 'The Sailor's Arms' it read. An inn! Exactly what I needed. A few seconds' further exploration showed me that the hotel's double gateway led into a courtyard.

I staggered back to the Landrover, managed to get the engine started, and, with the headlights on high beam, drove into the hotel yard. I grabbed my travelling bag, locked Sam's Landrover, and ran out of the rain through the first door I saw.

I found myself, dripping rain water, and battling for breath, in a small saloon bar. There was an open fireplace, a scattering of tables and chairs, and a bar across the end of the room. There were only two customers, sailors by the look of their oilskin coats, hunched over drinks at a corner table. When I walked in they looked up at me, glanced at each other, and then returned to their drinking.

Behind the bar was a fat-faced, middle-aged, jolly looking woman. 'Goodness gracious! Look at what the storm's blown in,' she cried.

'I'm sorry to be dripping all over your floor,' I said, still slightly out of breath.

'Oh, don't you worry about that, dearie, don't you worry about that. Just get that wet jacket of yours off, and sit down by the fire, while I make you a rum toddy. That's just the thing you need.'

She took my jacket and hung it over the back of a chair turned towards the fire to dry. Then she waddled off to make the rum toddy. I watched her splash a generous tot of real Phoenician rum into a glass, add a squeeze of lemon juice, and then top it up with hot water from the kettle on the hob. She smiled widely at the two customers in the corner as she passed.

'Get that into you, dearie,' she said as she handed me the drink.

And I did. The hot rum burnt all the way down, and then started a small volcano in my stomach, but it did me a power of good.

Then the woman (the publican's wife?) came and sat down beside me in front of the fire. 'What on earth possessed you to be out in this weather, dearie?' she asked.

'I'm on the way to Bethsaida,' I explained, 'and I got caught in the storm. I thought it might be safer to put up for the night in Tiberias.'

'Have another sip of your rum, my dearie, and tell Aunt Chloe—that's what everyone calls me—why you'd be making such a long journey.'

So I told her. Maybe it was the rum that loosened my tongue. Maybe she was such a sympathetic, motherly soul that I wanted to tell her. Maybe a little of both. I told her about the vanishing corpse, and about being hired by Big Joe Caiaphas. I told her about my investigation, and about how difficult I was finding it to pin down any hard facts. She nodded and listened, and halfway through my tale she made me another rum toddy.

What I failed to notice was, that as soon as I

started to talk, one of the oilskin-coated customers in the corner had quietly slipped out the door. If I had had my wits about me I would have wondered why a sailor would walk out into weather like that, when it was clear that no boats could be setting sail. When he came back, I did notice and I was still talking.

'And then...when I left Nazareth,' I yawned, '...when I left Nazareth...why am I getting so sleepy?'

'It's driving through the storm that's tired you out, dearie,' said Aunt Chloe. 'Have another sip of rum.'

I looked down at the glass in my hand, and suddenly my befuddled brain was stabbed by suspicion. 'There's something...in the drink,' I mumbled. 'Something... in...the drink...'

I tried to push myself to my feet. The floor seemed to have taken it into its head to waltz with the wind. It was tossing and rocking beneath my feet like a boat battling breakers. I put out a hand to steady myself.

Then I noticed that the two customers in oilskin coats were walking towards me. Aunt Chloe turned towards them.

'I thought you two boys might be interested in the stranger,' she said, or, at least, I think that's what she said. My ears seemed to have gone as out of focus as my eyes.

Quite abruptly I could cope with the pitching, heaving floor no longer, and collapsed into my chair. The two customers came and stood over me.

'Usual fee for my kindly assistance?' asked Aunt Chloe.

One of the men dug into his jacket, pulled out a gold coin, and dropped it into her outstretched hand.

Then he and his friend grabbed me by my arms and pulled me to my feet.

'Hey...hey...who...are...you...guys...?' I tried to protest.

They ignored my question, but as they manhandled me, one of the oilskin coats was pushed aside, and I caught a glimpse of a heavy leather jacket underneath. And, in a shoulder holster under the leather, the dull, blue gunmetal sheen of a four-five calibre automatic.

Then I understood. The leather jacket, the automatic in the shoulder holster gave it away. These guys were KBG, members of Herod's own King's Body Guard, the most vicious secret police in the whole of Judaea.

Chapter 27

When I came to, I was lying on a small bunk in a narrow room. For a moment my head swam: where was I? Who was I? What was I doing here?

Then it came back to me: 'The Sailor's Arms' and Aunt Chloe and the KBG men. I remembered being dragged out to the street and thrown into the back of a large, black limousine. Then I must have passed out.

I sat up. It was a mistake. A sharp pain shot through my head, and the room began to spin around. When the pain had subsided I slowly and cautiously raised myself to a sitting position again. By moving gently I could keep the pain in my head down to only mildly blinding.

The room had white plastered walls, one door, and one small window. Under the window were a plain wooden table and chair. I stood up—very slowly so as not to aggravate the throbbing acre of pain I mistakenly thought of as my head. I tried the door— it was locked. I checked the window—it was barred.

Beyond the bars patches of stars in the night sky told me that the clouds were breaking up. In fact, the rain and electrical storm had stopped, leaving only a howling, whistling wind outside. By standing on the chair I could make out the moon close to the horizon. I guessed the time to be somewhere between midnight and 2 am.

On the table was a jug of water and a glass. I sniffed at the water suspiciously. It seemed to be all right. I poured out a glass and took a small sip. It tasted like water, so I drank two large glassfulls. My mouth was like the bottom of a bird cage, and judging from the taste, the cage was occupied by an elderly, diseased parrot. I splashed some of the water on my face, in an attempt to clear my foggy brain, and ran my fingers through my hair.

My movement around the room must have made some noise because a small panel in the door slid open and a pair of eyes peered in. This was followed by the clanking of keys and the opening of the door.

Standing in the doorway was one of the KBG men. Divested of his oilskin raincoat he looked very large and threatening in his shiny, black leather jacket.

'Sleeping Beauty has woken up,' he growled, without, apparently, moving his lips.

'Ahoowie,' I said, which somewhat surprised me, since I was trying to make some smart remark about my Handsome Prince having woken me up, but all I managed was, *'Ahoowie'.* It appeared that my brain and mouth were not quite back into gear.

'Come along,' growled Leatherjacket, in his ventriloquist fashion. 'Herod wanted to see you as soon as you woke up. Let's go.'

Herod? My prison cell, then, was in Herod's palace. Up endless staircases, and down long corridors I

173

was dragged by my jailer, and the furniture and fittings become more elaborate and ornate the closer we got to Herod's quarters.

After a few minutes we were facing a huge double door, elaborately carved out of Lebanese cedar. From beyond the door music was drifting. Leatherjacket pushed the door open, and it swung back noiselessly and smoothly to reveal a large, high-ceilinged banqueting room.

We walked in through the door, which my guard closed behind us, and down the length of the ornate chamber. On our way we had to avoid the richly dressed guests who were sprawled out sleeping on couches and cushions.

At the end of the room a few people were still awake, eating, drinking and talking in a desultory fashion. In the centre of the group, on the largest and most ornate couch, were a man and a woman—King Herod, and his queen, Herodias. It was the queen I noticed first. She was beautiful. Although old enough to have a teenage daughter, she was still quite young herself, and still had that legendary beauty. She was Herod's niece as well as his wife. In fact, she had made a career of marrying uncles, first marrying her Uncle Philip, and then Philip's more odious brother Herod.

As we approached she stared at me appraisingly, through lowered eyelids.

Herod looked up as my guard spoke: 'The detective from Jerusalem, Your Majesty. You wished to see him when he regained consciousness.'

'So I did, so I did,' said the King languorously.

Herod reminded me of a feral animal. His long, thin, bony face and small, sharp, darting eyes suggested a fox. An old, cunning fox. His bony face managed to combine an appearance of cadaverous illness, with a puffiness around the eyes and lips that spoke of unrestrained self-indulgence.

'Come a little closer, detective,' he said in a soft and sibilant voice.

I took a step closer.

'Your story has been told to me. You have come into my kingdom to find a corpse, I am told. Is this correct?'

'Yes,' I said.

'I beg your pardon?'

'Yes, that's correct.'

The KBG man behind me suddenly grabbed my shoulders and pushed me down hard, banging my knees onto the marble floor.

'Have you never spoken to a king before?' asked Herod.

'No,' I gasped. The KBG man was still gripping my shoulders, and he was digging his thumbs painfully into my muscles.

'Then I suppose we must forgive your ignorant, lower class manners. The correct form of address is "Your Majesty". Understood?'

'Yes...er, yes, Your Majesty.'

'That's better.'

The KBG man released his grip, and I took a deep breath.

'Now, young man, when you, or anyone else, comes into my kingdom on a matter of official business I expect that, as a matter of courtesy, your first call would be upon the palace, to explain your presence and ask permission for your search. You have been less than polite in this matter, have you not?'

'I'm afraid so, Your Majesty, I'm sorry about that. It never occurred to me that you might be interested in my investigation—Your Majesty.'

'Well I am...a little. I don't like the chief priests

in Jerusalem. They are so censorious. And so ungrateful. Do you like them, young man?'

'Well . . .'

'I take it that you don't. Good. Good. My father built that temple of theirs for them, and they have never shown one minute's gratitude. Not one minute's. So, I am always pleased when I can frustrate any of their little plans.'

He paused to take a long drink from a golden goblet that he held limply in his bejewelled, ring-splattered left hand.

'Now, the question is,' murmured Herod, talking more to himself than to me, 'how I can most effectively frustrate them. Perhaps, it would be simplest to just eliminate you.'

'Your Majesty!' I spluttered, rapidly wishing I had never met Shagmar or heard of the Jesus Movement.

Herod gestured me to silence with a wave of his hand. 'Or, perhaps, I can send you back to them with some entirely misleading information?' He leaned over and whispered in his wife's ear. She giggled and whispered back.

Herod paused to take another drink, and then continued, 'I remember this Jesus. He seemed a harmless enough fellow, although rather lacking in manners, like yourself, young man. Why did they have him killed?'

'They were afraid of his popularity,' hissed Herodias, with a wicked gleam in her eye, 'afraid of an armed insurrection by his followers.'

'That's right,' said Herod, his face lighting up with cunning. 'If they are afraid of an insurrection, let's give them one. They sent you up here to find his followers, didn't they?'

'Yes—Your Majesty.'

176

'Then you will say that you found them. And that they are arming for an insurrection, to avenge their leader's death. Tell them that hundreds of wild Galilean fishermen, armed to the teeth, are descending on Jerusalem to tear the city apart.'

Herod laughed. A vicious, nasty laugh. 'All the nervous nellies in the temple, Caiaphas, old Annas, and the rest, will give birth to kittens just thinking about it.'

Queen Herodias, now giggling drunkenly, leaned over and whispered something in the king's ear.

'Wonderful, my dear! Simply wonderful!' cried Herod in delight. 'You have a truly wicked imagination. Young man, you will ring Caiaphas with the news. Now. At two o'clock in the morning.'

'But—Your Majesty—'

'Just make the phone call—or you die.'

(And if I do make the phone call, I thought, when I get back to Jerusalem, Caiaphas will have me killed anyway.)

Herod was paying no attention to my torment; he was giggling again at the ingenuity of his scheme. 'If Caiaphas is woken up now, in the early hours of the morning, and told now, while he is still half asleep, that a wild band of heavily armed Galileans is descending on his temple to kill him in revenge for the death of their master, he will die of fright! Absolutely die! Oh, what a delicious thought.'

While I thought fast, Herod clapped his hands and called for a telephone. What could I do? If I refused to make the phone-call Herod would have me killed on the spot. But if I made it, once Caiaphas discovered that it was false he would send Shagmar to kill me, no matter where I hid. What should I do?

'Dial the number!' ordered Herod when the telephone arrived.

I hesitated. Then I felt the cold, hard metal of a KBG gun barrel being pressed into the back of my neck. I picked up the telephone.

'This is going to be wonderful!' gloated Herod.

Then I had an idea. 'I have to check the number,' I said, and I fished in my pocket for the business card the RIA had given me. And that was the number I dialled hoping and praying that it was an emergency number that the RIA man had switched through to his room when he went to bed. It was.

'Hello?' said a sleepy voice at the other end.

'Sorry to wake you,' I said. 'It's Bartholomew. You told me to ring this number if I needed to talk to you.'

'Oh, yeah, Bartholomew. What do you want at this time in the morning?'

'Well, I'm calling from the palace of King Herod.' Then I swallowed hard and said, 'I want you to talk to him about my investigation—that is, if you want it to go ahead?'

'Sure we want it to go ahead—you're our window into possible political unrest. Put him on.'

While this was going on, Herod was looking more and more puzzled.

I held out the phone. 'He wants to speak to you,' I said, and gave the handpiece to the king.

The puzzlement turned to anger, as Herod grabbed the phone from my hand, and snapped, 'Yes?' down the line.

I couldn't hear what the RIA man said to Herod, but I saw that it made him pale with anger, and then paler still with fear. I had guessed correctly: the only power Herod feared was Roman power. Without Roman protection he would cease to be king.

The RIA man's voice was a thin tinkling coming out of the earpiece. I could make out only a few words: '...will I wake up Pilate?' But that was enough.

After several minutes Herod hung up the phone. He then cursed the Romans up hill and down dale for five solid minutes, using a collection of scatalogical, reproductive, and theological terms in a manner entirely unrelated to their literal meanings.

When he'd finished he turned towards me. Now I'm for it, I thought. But it turned out that the protection of Rome extended, at least for the moment, to my person.

'Throw him out!' snarled the king. 'Take him back where you picked him up, and leave him there!'

Chapter 28

So, there I stood, in the early hours of the morning, in front of 'The Sailor's Arms' with the KBG limousine roaring off down the street. The rain had stopped, but the street was still awash with storm water, and the savage wind that howled and whistled off the lake chilled me to the bone. I pushed open the front door and stepped into the saloon bar of the small inn.

The scene was almost unchanged from the night before, except that there were now no customers, and 'Aunt Chloe' was lolling in a chair in front of the fire in a drunken sleep. As she slept she snored loudly.

I walked behind the bar, and got myself a stiff shot of brandy. Then I did some exploring. In the kitchen behind the bar I fixed myself some bread and cheese and a large mug of coffee. While I was there I packed a bag full of food to take on the road: fresh fruit, salted beef, cheese, a loaf of bread and a small bottle of wine.

From a small private sitting room behind the kitchen I took a thick, woollen rug.

Back in the saloon bar I found my jacket and travelling bag exactly where I had left them. I left the inn through the yard, and there was Sam's Landrover—looking like a home away from home. In the corner of the yard were several drums of petrol, so I topped up the Landrover's tank, threw the travelling bag and rug onto the front seat beside me, started up the vehicle, and drove out the gate.

By now it was some time after 3 am as I retraced my path through the town. Tiberias had clearly been a mistake, and I had no intention of staying one minute longer than necessary.

With the rain gone, and the moon out, navigating my way through the dark streets was much easier than it had been the night before. Once outside the city wall, I turned right, and headed north up the road along the lake. When Tiberias was out of sight, I drove off the road under some overhanging branches where the Landrover would be less visible.

Then I made sure all the doors were locked securely, wrapped the thick woollen rug around me, and went to sleep.

I slept the sleep of the just and utterly exhausted, and the sun was well up by the time I woke. I breakfasted on some of the food from 'The Sailor's Arms', and then walked a hundred yards down to the shore of the lake to wash in the stingingly cold water. Back at the Landrover I changed my shirt and brushed my hair, and then set out for Bethsaida. It was not far, and I knew I could be there by nightfall.

All signs of yesterday's storm were gone, leaving blue skies, and fresh breezes blowing in off the lake full of ozone and seaweed. Exactly what I needed to rinse the sickly aroma of Herod's palace out of my mind. Herod, I decided, was like a rotting carcass on which gallons of perfume had been splashed in an attempt to smother the smell of decay.

But that was behind me now. I was glad now, as I had not been in Jerusalem, that the Romans had decided to take an interest in the case and use me as their eyes and ears. I could do with the protection.

As I drove on, with the wind whistling cheerfully through the car, I began to feel that I was getting somewhere with my investigation.

Lunch time found me in Magdala, with its famous fish-pickling factory on the outskirts. Stacked outside the factory were those familiar barrels of pickled fish labelled 'Product of Galilee' that could be found in any market in Jerusalem. In the middle of the town I parked the car and found a small cafe. I always like to eat the local delicacy—so I ordered salad and pickled fish.

After lunch, and a walk around the town square to stretch my legs, I climbed back into the Landrover and resumed the northward journey.

On the outskirts of Magdala I saw a hitch-hiker standing by the side of the road. He looked like a nice enough young man, so I pulled over.

'How far are you going?' he asked.

'Bethsaida.'

'That's where I'm heading,' he said. 'You don't mind a passenger?'

'Hop in.'

He climbed in the passenger's seat and then offered me his hand, 'Tom's the name,' he said.

'Ben,' I said, as I shook his hand. 'I reckon we'll be in Bethsaida by nightfall.'

'Oh, I doubt it,' he said, although I couldn't understand why.

Chapter 29

Sam's old Landrover was now firing well, and we were making good speed. The only clouds that warm, sunny afternoon were white, puffy ones to the north.

'Well, Tom,' I said, 'it looks as though that storm is well and truly gone.'

My passenger scanned the skies for a minute or two. 'I doubt it,' he said.

'Oh well, you could be right,' I admitted. 'I don't know this part of the world all that well. You from around here?'

'Born here. Grew up here,' said Tom.

'Why are you going back now?'

'I'm due at a meeting. In fact, I should have been there a week ago, but I sprained an ankle and I couldn't travel. I have a bit of a reputation for that,' he added ruefully. 'Missing meetings, that is.'

'You have my sympathy—I'm not all that punctual myself.'

For a while we drove in silence.

'This old Landrover,' I said, just to make conversation, 'is over ten years old, but the way it's running now, I would not be surprised if my friend Sam gets another ten years out of it.'

'Ten years?' said Tom. 'I doubt it.'

'Perhaps you're right. Maybe five years would be more like it.'

'Five is more feasible, but, still, I doubt it.'

'You're a real sceptic, aren't you?'

'We both are. My brother and I, that is. We're twins, identical twins. Strangers say they can't pick Tim and me apart.'

' "Tim" and "Tom"? Confusing names for identical twins.'

'Yes, when we were kids in school whichever name the teacher called out, we'd both answer—and, of course, she couldn't tell which was which.'

'I think I'd be able to tell you apart—if I saw you and Tim together, that is. I'm a trained observer. I did a course on it once. I'm supposed to be able to pick up small differences.'

'And you think you could pick us apart?'

'Yes.'

'I doubt it.'

For the next ten minutes we drove in silence.

After a while he asked, 'Why are you up this way?'

By way of reply I dug into my top pocket, pulled out my P.I.'s licence, and flashed it at him.

'Ah, I see. That's what you meant by the "trained observer" stuff. You on a case?'

'That's right. A theft case. The temple authorities have hired me to find the body of Jesus the Nazarene—the corpse is missing from the tomb it was buried in three weeks ago.'

'And are you making any progress?' Suddenly he

sounded more interested. I could tell he was not making small talk any longer.

'It's a bit like trying to run in wet sand. But I'm a determined investigator. I'll find it.'

This time he laughed, actually laughed out loud. 'I doubt it,' he laughed. 'I doubt it.'

'All right, Mr Sceptic,' I said through clenched teeth. 'Since you're so smart. Why do you doubt it? Why won't I find the corpse?'

'Because it's not there to be found. There is no corpse.'

'Explain yourself.'

'I am part of the movement, I am one of his friends. And I know that Jesus has done what he set out to do. He has conquered the last enemy: death.'

It was clear that I was going to get the same story I had got from Cleopas and from Jim Davidson.

'And you believe all that?' I asked.

'I don't believe it, I know it. When the others said they had seen Jesus, I scoffed, I refused to believe them.'

'Let me guess... You said, "I doubt it". Right?'

'Right. I told them that seeing wouldn't be good enough for me. Unless I could touch the resurrected body of Jesus I would not believe. A week later we were together, and suddenly Jesus was there with us.'

Tom's voice had gone quiet. And he was staring straight ahead, looking at a memory instead of the scenery.

'He was there with us, just as real and as solid as you or me. "Peace be with you," he said, just as he had so often before his death. Then he turned to me and said, "Touch me. Stretch out your hand and touch me. Stop your doubting and believe!" And his voice was just as loud and just as real as your voice.'

'And what did you say?'

'What do you expect? The wind was knocked right out of my sails, all I could gasp out was, "My Lord and my God!" And Jesus touched me. He put his hand on my shoulder and said to me, "Do you believe because you see me? How happy are those who believe without seeing me!"'

Just then the road rounded a corner and we found ourselves in the little lakeside town of Gennesaret. Unfortunately, I had to stop at a service station to buy petrol, but we were soon back on the road again, and I reopened the subject.

'Listen, Tom, I need to find your friends in Bethsaida. Will you help me?'

'I don't mind helping. We have nothing to hide.'

'Is there a meeting place, a sort of base, in Bethsaida?'

'Yes, there is. It's the house of old Zebedee Boanerges. That's where I'm going.'

'Is Zebedee a member of the movement too?'

'Yep. And so is his wife, and so are their two sons, John and Jim. Mind you, it took Old Zeb a while to sort of get a handle on it all. After all, Jesus was, or is, Zeb's nephew, and I guess it's a little hard to get hold of the idea that your nephew is the rescuer of the world.'

'I guess so. So, he's the uncle of Jesus?'

'Yep. Old Zeb's wife is Salome, a nice old bird and one of the best cooks in the whole of Galilee. Anyway, Sal's the sister of Mary the mother of Jesus.'

'And where can I find this house?'

'I'll take you there.'

'And one other thing. I was told that the movement is run by a board of directors, or council, or something, called the Eleven. How do I find them?'

'You've found them, Ben. I am one of the Eleven.'

The news silenced me for a bit. Having this hardened sceptic turn out to be a true believer was difficult enough to cope with, discovering that he was also one of the leaders made it worse. I guess I'd been expecting leaders who were devious and manipulative, not leaders who, like Tom, were transparent in their belief, and honest about their own scepticism.

'So you're one of the leaders of the Jesus Movement?'

'Well, one of the Eleven, yes.'

'Are you certain that you're not being fooled about this vanishing corpse business? I mean, couldn't one of the others have stolen the corpse—without telling you?'

'Who? Peter? John? Matthew? No! They're plain men, even simple men. They're tradesmen, and fishermen, and minor public servants. They're not great schemers. And I've known all of them for at least three years. If one of them had somehow got rid of the body, and faked the empty tomb, I would know.'

Yes, I thought, I suppose you would, Tom. If anyone would, you would pick it up.

'But that's not the real point,' Tom continued. 'I've seen Jesus. So have others. Lots of others. Ask any of them. They didn't see a ghost, or an illusion, or have a group hallucination. What I have been telling you is true. Jesus has conquered death. He's back!'

'And you have no doubts about that?'

'I don't doubt it for a minute!'

The road was now curving around the edge of the lake and taking us in a north-easterly direction. Shortly after sunset it became apparent that we would not make it into Bethsaida until well after the evening meal hour was over. Tom didn't seem to have eaten all day so I parked by the edge of the lake and dug out the last of the food I had "borrowed" from the Sailor's Arms. The bread was still quite fresh, and there was plenty of cheese, and salted beef, and fruit. Tom started a fire to boil water and we finished the meal with hot coffee, and the last of the wine. Then we extinguished the fire, repacked the Landrover, and set off for the last hour or two of the journey into Bethsaida.

Just after sunset we passed through Capernaum, another fishing town with a Roman garrison on the outskirts, and dominated by a handsome new synagogue on a hill overlooking the town. After Capernaum, the road followed the curve of the lake shore.

An hour later our destination showed up as a row of lights upon the horizon, and I pushed my foot down hard on the accelerator, to eat up the last few miles as quickly as possible.

Soon we were driving past a scattering of houses on the outskirts of Bethsaida, and Tom started giving directions. An assortment of "lefts" and "next rights" took us to a street that rose to a small hill overlooking the main body of the town. Tom directed me to stop in front of a large family villa, close to the local synagogue.

'This is it,' said Tom.

Chapter 30

'I'll let you off, Tom,' I said, 'and go and find some accommodation.'

'Nonsense! Come inside with me. Zeb and Sal have plenty of spare rooms, I'm sure they can put you up.'

'No, no. I don't want to be a nuisance. I'll go into town and find a motel or something.'

'I doubt that. Everything closes early in Bethsaida. Stay here. I know the Boanerges family well enough to know they will make you more than welcome.'

'Are you sure?'

'Quite sure! I know Old Zeb. And when I know someone I have no doubts about them.'

'Okay, I'll just come in and see.'

We mounted stone steps to a porch set in an impressive colonnade, and Tom rapped on a large, bronze door knocker.

The door was opened by the household steward (a sort of senior servant).

'Can I help you?' he asked, in a plum-in-the-mouth voice.

'Tell Zebedee that Tom Didymus is here. And tell him I have brought a friend with me.'

'Certainly, gentlemen. If you'll step this way.'

He conducted us inside. The house was square, two storeys high, built round a large courtyard. The courtyard itself contained several palm trees and a well. We were invited to sit on cedar benches underneath the palm trees while the servant conveyed Tom's message to the interior of the villa.

'An impressive house,' I said to Tom, as I looked around.

'The Boanerges are a fishing family,' he explained. 'Old Zeb, and his father before him, expanded the business so that nowadays they run a small fleet of fishing boats and a fish wholesaling company as well.'

As we sat there my nose told me we were not alone in the courtyard. Looking around I discovered that we shared it with a flock of chickens, a goat, and several sheep! I reminded myself that although I was a city boy, I could live quite comfortably with the more bucolic elements of civilisation.

After a few minutes the servant returned, and with him came a short, weather-beaten, nuggety man, with a bald head and a big grin.

'Tom!' he cried. 'We expected you a week ago.'

'I injured my ankle and couldn't travel. Are the others here?'

'No. They were summoned to a meeting further up the mountain, up towards Chorazin.'

'Summoned? You mean by the Master?'

'That's who. He met them by the lakeside and told them to bring the disciples to the old meeting place on the mountain.'

'But you didn't go?'

'Someone has to jolly well keep an eye on the house, and on the business. So, I volunteered. Sal's gone with them, she'll tell me all about it. Tom, introduce me to your friend.'

'Oops, sorry about that. Zebedee, I'd like you to meet my friend and chauffeur (and Private Detective)' said Tom. 'And Ben, I must apologise, I've been neglecting you. Zebedee, meet Ben Bartholomew, Ben—Zebedee Boanerges.'

'I'm pleased to meet you, Mr Boanerges.'

'Call me Zeb. Everyone does,' he said with a grin, shaking my hand as he spoke (his hand felt like leather). 'A jolly detective, eh?'

'Ben picked me up just outside Magdala when I was trying to hitch-hike my way up here,' continued Tom. 'He has been hired by the temple authorities to track down the missing corpse of Jesus Davidson!'

'That's jolly interesting,' said Zeb. 'I'd like to hear, Ben, how your investigation is going.'

'Ben's looking for accommodation, Zebedee. Can you help?' said Tom.

'Of course! You must both stay here, tonight and for as many nights as you need. There are plenty of spare rooms, and I shall be jolly grateful to have you. Until Sal and the boys come back, I only have the servants for company.'

'Thank you,' I said, gratefully, but Tom insisted that he could only stay the night. 'First thing tomorrow I must find the others.'

'Are you sure you won't wait here for them, Tom? They are due back in a few days time.'

'No, I'd like to be with them as soon as possible.'

'As for you, Ben,' said Zebedee, 'you stay here with me for a few days. You can pursue your investigations with the Eleven, and the rest of the disciples, when they return. In the meantime, you can tell me of your investigations. I've never met a jolly detective before.'

Then Zeb sent a couple of servants to fetch our bags from the Landrover, directing Tom's to his 'usual room' and mine to the upstairs corner bedroom.

Then, with a clap of his hands, he summoned the household steward. 'Ephraim, wine for our guests.'

The three of us sat at a small table, underneath one of the carriage lamps that lit the courtyard. Ephraim poured wine from a jug into our goblets, and we drank in silence for a little. Then Tom asked, 'How's the business going these days, Zeb?'

'I shouldn't grumble, but it's jolly hard to find good workers these days, Tom. There's one boat I just can't find a crew for at all. Today's young blokes don't seem interested in hard work. But you don't want to hear about my troubles. We'd better see about getting you two settled.'

A servant was assigned to Tom, and another one to me, to show us to our rooms and to unpack our things.

'You two will want a jolly good night's sleep after your long day's travel,' said Zebedee, 'so I'll say goodnight, and I'll see you in the morning.'

My room was square and sparsely furnished. As I looked around, the servant arrived, carrying a jug of water, a basin and a towel. He placed them on a low table, next to the bed.

As he was doing this I took a close look at him. He was certainly an odd-looking servant. Most servants in Judaea and Galilee are Jews. And they look like Jews. A few of them are Greeks (usually employed as private secretaries). And they look like Greeks.

This guy looked like neither. In fact, with his broad nose, his weathered face, and his close-cropped hair, he looked exactly like a Roman soldier. 'But,' I said to myself, 'what would a Roman soldier be doing, dressed like a slave, and doing the work of a servant? Even the lowest Roman trooper regards himself as superior to all the conquered races. So, no Roman soldier would ever let himself sink to their level by working as a servant.'

I looked at him more closely, completely baffled. Then, like a flash of lightning, it hit me.

I waited until he was about to leave the room, and then I called sharply, 'Publius!'

He froze where he stood, and turned slowly to face me.

'You *are* Julius Publius, aren't you?'

He did not reply. He stood there silent and sullen.

'Magnus Cassius told me to find you,' I said.

That changed matters, and his face softened. 'Yes,' he said, 'I am Publius.'

'Does Zebedee know that you are a deserter?'

'Yes. I told him my whole story.'

'And he knows what he is taking on, in sheltering a deserter?'

'He understands. It was Salome who offered to take me. But Zebedee agreed to it. He is a man of open mind and generous heart.'

'And you have told all these people your story?'

'Yes, I have.'

'Sit down, Publius. I'd like you to tell it to me, please.'

Chapter 31

The bed was a thin, wool-filled mattress spread out on the floor. I squatted on it, and Publius sat on the wooden stool.

'How much has Marcus told you?' he asked.

'Enough. Enough to know whether you're lying to me or not. So, what's your version of events? What happened in that garden, outside the tomb, on that Sunday morning?'

His eyes sort of drifted out of focus as he lost himself in memory. . . 'It was my last active duty for the Roman army, although, at the time, I didn't know it was going to be. It started out in boredom, and ended in sheer terror.'

He paused to think for a moment, and then asked, 'Have you ever seen an angel?'

(Why are people always asking me if I've seen an angel?)

'No', I said, once more, 'I've never seen an angel.'

'I have, that morning at the tomb. Cassius and I both saw an angel. Frightened the life out of us it did.

Mind you, young Cassius and I only worked out afterwards that what he was an angel. What he looked like was a young man, a young man dressed all in white. It was what he did that impressed us. Although there was something special about his appearance too. He looked as though he was standing in a pool of bright, blue-white moonlight. Afterwards, when I remembered that the moon wasn't up at the time, I realised why his appearance was so unearthly. I keep calling him "he"—are angels "he"? I'm not sure. I'm sorry, I'm not telling this very well.'

'You just tell it like it was,' I said. 'I can sort it out as I listen.'

'Okay. Well, he came during the earthquake. Do you know about the earthquake?'

'Yes, I know.'

'That's when he came. When the earth was trembling. Marcus Cassius and I looked up and we both saw him. We had been sitting beside a little fire that we had built to keep us warm. The night had been very quiet and still, and we had passed the time playing cards. It was very boring. Night shifts on guard duty are always boring. The priests from the temple had sealed the tomb and left us quite early the night before.'

'What do you call early?'

'Oh, an hour after sunset, not any later than that. And the priests weren't there for long. They just sealed the stone with a wax seal, so they could tell in the morning if it had been tampered with, and left.'

'Any chance that the tomb had been tampered with before you arrived?'

'I don't think so. At any rate, there were certainly no signs that it had been tampered with. The stone was solidly in place, and the ground around it was undisturbed. So. . . Where was I? Oh yes, Cassius and I built a fire and sat around it talking and playing cards, bored out of our brains. Then there was this earthquake. Well, just a sort of tremor, really. And then we saw the angel. Or rather, the young man who we later worked out was an angel.'

'Where was he?'

'Standing right in front of the tomb. And it's what he did, more than how he looked, that convinced us he was an angel. He rolled away the stone. That's what he did. That's how the stone was moved. That's how the tomb was opened. He rolled away the stone. Just this young man dressed in white. . .alone, with one hand. He pushed back that giant stone like it was a child's toy. And then—he sat on it. He rolled it away and then climbed up and sat on it. It was as though he was displaying a kind of amused contempt for all the precautions and security that mere human beings could contrive.'

'That was the impression you got at the time?'

'Behind the primary feeling of sheer terror, that was the impression, yes.'

'Now, you and Marcus Cassius were soldiers, Roman soldiers, sent to guard that tomb. Did you challenge this young man?'

'It wasn't like that. We were terrified. We actually shook with fear. Seeing the angel roll away that huge stone frightened us. It was uncanny. It was unearthly.' Publius's voice fell to little more than a whisper. 'Cassius and I were so terrified, for a while we were like dead men. Then we ran away to a distant corner of the garden to hide.'

'Did you see anyone come out of the tomb?'

'No.'

'Did you see anyone go in?'

'Not then. Later.'

'Who?'

'First, there was the woman. I know now that it was Mary Magdalene. I've met her, here in Zebedee's house. She was the first. She came into the garden, walking slowly, in tears. And a minute later she ran away again, in a panic. She can't have been at the tomb any time at all.'

This was starting to sound familiar. But I wanted to hear it again. I was looking for contradictions, for evidence that this was fiction, not fact.

'But there were others,' I said. 'Tell me about the others.'

'After the first woman, there was a group of women. I know now that Sal was one of them, together with another Mary and a woman I haven't met, by the name of Joanna. They went up to the tomb. They were there for longer. When they came back they were talking and laughing. They were happy.'

Publius's voice was getting stronger. He was speaking with confidence and certainty.

'Then there were two men. One of them was Peter, although I didn't know it then, and the other was John, Zeb's son. They ran into the garden. Running and out of breath they were. They also were at the tomb for some time. And when they came back past where Cassius and I were hiding they had their heads together, deep in conversation. Then Mary Magdalene came back again. She was there for a while, and then she left. There was no one else. And the garden was quiet again. So Cassius and I crept out of our hiding place, and back to the tomb. We looked inside, or, at least, I did. Poor young Magnus's nerves were starting to come apart by this. So I looked inside—and the tomb was empty!'

'With all this coming and going, could any of those people have been carrying a body when they left?'

'No. Cassius and I could see them as plainly as I can see you now. All of them. No one was carrying a body. Not the women. Not the two men. No one.'

'You absolutely sure?'

'Absolutely. We watched them come in and we watched them go out. No one stole a body. Magnus Cassius and I were together. We could see clearly from where we were. No one took a body.'

'Look, it's all quite clear in my mind,' he said with some exasperation. 'It was only three weeks ago, and I remember it exactly: the young man in white who rolled away the stone; Mary Magdalene coming and going and then returning later; the group of three women who came and went; and Peter and John who also came and went—and I saw no one steal a corpse, not the young man in white who opened the tomb, not Peter and John, not the three women, not Mary Magdalene. And yet, after they had left, I looked in the tomb—and it was empty!'

'So, what did you and Private Cassius do?'

'We reported what we had seen to the priests.'

'Everything?'

'Everything. They made us go over the details again and again. I think they may even have sent two of the temple guards down to the garden to check out our story. But, of course, by then the garden was deserted—and so was the tomb. They were as baffled as we were. They had us wait in a room by ourselves while they worked out what to do. By this time my nerves had got over the shock, but poor young Magnus had sort of gone to pieces. He looked pale and ill. After a while they came and got us and took us in to see the boss—Caiaphas himself. He told us we were to say that Jesus' friends had come during the night and stolen him away while we were asleep. I protested that we'd be lashed and thrown into the guardhouse, with a story like that. But Caiaphas insisted that he would put it right with the governor, and, anyway, Cassius was nodding his head and prepared to go along with anything Caiaphas wanted. So I said I'd go along with it too. As long as we didn't get into trouble over it. And then Caiaphas sat down and wrote out a cheque for each of us—a substantial cheque I can tell you. As he handed them over he said, "Some glue to keep your mouths fastened". Well, Cassius and I grabbed the money and got out of there as quickly as we could.'

'And did you spread the story that Caiaphas had paid you to spread?'

'If anyone asked me I told them Caiaphas's story, and I swore it was true. But if people didn't ask, I didn't bother. I made no real effort to spread the story. But I gather that it got around a bit of its own accord. Maybe the priests were spreading it, I don't know. Magnus Cassius didn't, I know that. He took to his bed in nervous prostration.'

'But that's not the end of the story, is it?'

'What do you mean?'

'You still have to explain how you come to be here.'

Chapter 32

'That's the simplest part. There's really nothing to it. I had several days leave due. And I spent them trying to figure it all out. Since I'd been based in Jerusalem I'd taken an interest in the Jewish religion, and I'd found their pure form of monotheism attractive. Or, at least, intellectually cohesive and reasonable. And I'd read in the *Jerusalem Times* that the temple authorities had sentenced Jesus to death for blasphemy—claiming to be God, or claiming that he and God were of one substance, something like that. For a pure monotheist that sort of claim has to be the worst heresy. But what if it was true?

'If Jesus was who and what he claimed to be, then death could never have held him in its clutches for long, and what I had seen made sense. So, I decided to track down his followers. It took me a couple of days to locate them, and when I did, and talked to them, it turned out that what I had experienced, and what they had experienced, fitted together and made the story complete.'

'But, why didn't you then just go back to soldiering when your leave was over?'

'Don't you see? If all this is untrue then it doesn't matter. But if it is true it matters enormously. The one thing it cannot be is true and unimportant. Well, I'm convinced it's true, so I took the risk of deserting and throwing in my lot with these people.'

'And what will you do now?'

'Probably stay up here in Galilee. I can't risk returning to Jerusalem. Zeb's sons, John and Jim, have important work to do for the movement, and that leaves Zeb shorthanded. So, maybe I can stay here and help Zeb run the business.'

There was a short silence and then he asked, 'Are you going to turn me in?'

'No,' I said. 'It's not my job to chase deserters for the Roman army, and I'm not interested in seeing you punished.'

'Thanks,' he said. 'Thanks for that.'

Later that night as I lay on my thin mattress trying to sleep, I thought about Publius's story. His belief in its truth was obvious—just like Cleopas, and Jim Davidson, and Tom Didymus. But it still didn't satisfy me. What I wanted was a nice simple explanation for the whole thing. Nothing supernatural. Nothing unearthly. No God involved. Just a nice, simple, commonsense explanation. I fell asleep wrestling with the problem.

I deliberately made the next day a quiet one—resting, eating, chatting to Zeb. I had survived several very hectic, long, heavy days, and I reckoned I had earned a rest.

The day began early, because that thin mattress woke me up with the sparrows. Seeing I was awake, I decided to wash and dress and go for a walk in the cool, fresh early morning air. Maybe down to the edge of the lake where the fishing boats were moored, I thought.

There was only one other person stirring when I left my room, and that was Tom. 'Morning, Ben,' he said. 'Sleep well?'

'Not really,' I said.

'Ah, that'll be the mattress. You're too soft for this country life. None of your city luxuries here.'

We were both whispering, so as not to wake the household.

'I'm off up the mountain to find the others,' said Tom.

'Do you want to borrow the Landrover?'

'That's kind of you, Ben. But I have an old motorbike I left here when I went down to Jerusalem. It's a trail bike, and I can cut across country to catch up with the others.'

'Well, good luck. I hope you find them.'

A few minutes later a motorbike kicked into life at the back of the house. A little 150 cc by the sound of it. And then it was time for my morning walk.

I left the house quietly, so as not to disturb those who were still asleep, and found myself in a deserted street. Well, almost deserted. Just opposite the Boanerges' house, parked under a sycamore tree, was a small black car—a Peugeot sports car with tinted windows—and someone was sitting in it.

'Now who could he be waiting for at this hour of the morning?' I wondered.

Down at the lake I walked around the water's edge for half an hour, flinging pebbles out into the waves, and watching flocks of white storks winging their way across the waters, then I strolled back to the house.

The black car was still in the street, and its occupant was still in the driver's seat.

Inside, I found the house astir and breakfast being cooked. The car bothered me, so I asked Zeb to come to a front window to see if he could identify it.

'Does it belong to one of your neighbours? Have you ever seen it before?'

'The answers are, "no" and "no",' he replied.

'Certain?'

'Jolly certain!'

And that made me more uneasy.

Later in the morning I walked to the corner shop to buy a newspaper. The car was still there. For some time I stood on the street corner pretending to read the paper while surreptitiously observing the car and its occupant. By now he had rolled the car forward a little to stay in the shade of the sycamore, and had wound down his side window, presumably to keep the car a little cooler.

Through that open window, and over the top of my newspaper, I could just make out the driver's face. And I thought I recognised him. But at that distance I couldn't be sure. With the paper tucked under my arm I strolled casually towards the Peugeot. As I approached the driver turned his face away, as though passionately interested in something inside the car. Clearly, he was concerned that I might identify him.

Then I had a stroke of luck. A wasp flew into the car. For thirty seconds the occupant concentrated on shoo-ing the wasp away and I caught a good, clear look at his face. It was Shagmar's driver! It was the man who had driven the limo the day Shagmar had picked me up from in front of my office. And the man who, I believed, had murdered Barabbas!

I hurried inside the Boanerges house. Now I was

really worried. How had Shagmar tracked me here? And why was he keeping me on such a short rope? Shagmar's personal driver and hit-man was not sitting in a street in Bethsaida for his health! The threat was as obvious as a Gentile in a synagogue. Something nasty was being planned, and that gave me an uneasy feeling in the pit of my stomach.

One possibility occurred to me and I checked it out at once. I went out to the Landrover, and drove it around to the back of the house and went over it from back to front, checking every surface. I found what I was looking for underneath a rear mudguard—a small, oblong, black box. It was a beeper: a small, radio direction signal transmitter, powered by an inbuilt nickel-cadmium battery. Obviously, Shagmar had had it fitted before I even left Jerusalem. It would have been easy with the Landrover parked in the street. Equally obviously, he had never intended to trust me, and had been keeping me on a short lead the whole time.

But, until now, he hadn't bothered to put a man right on my heels. It looked as though the crunch was coming.

My first reaction was to throw the beeper down the well in Zeb's courtyard. But, on second thoughts, I decided it was better not to let them know, for the time being, that I had found it. The less they know about what I know, the better, I thought.

At the end of the day I was able to tell myself that it had been a quiet day, but an uneasy one. From now on I had to be on the alert, waiting for Shagmar to pull something unpleasant out of the bag.

Just on sunset, when the evening meal was being cooked and pleasant smells were drifting out of the kitchen, there was the sound of vehicles in the street, then voices and footsteps, then the front doors swung open and a whole mob of people crowded in. There must have been at least twenty of them.

For a moment I thought Shagmar had launched a raid on the house, and then I saw Tom in the crowd, and I saw that a good many of them were women, and that they were laughing and joking as they walked in. Then I realised who they were. These were the disciples, the crowd that Tom had gone to join earlier in the day.

Some of them I recognised from their descriptions. There was a tall, broad-shouldered man with flaming red hair and a booming laugh: I took him to be Peter. And there were two shorter, dark-haired men with loud voices. From the way they took over the place I guessed them to be John and Jim, Zebedee's sons. There was one pink-faced, white-haired woman who gave Zeb a hug and then headed off to the kitchen. I assumed that she was Salome.

And, in the heart of the crowd, laughing and talking with the rest, was someone who made my heart stand still. It was—Rachel!

Chapter 33

The last time I had seen Rachel had been... When? Two days ago? More? It had been in the heart of Jerusalem, getting on a bus for Galilee. And now, here she was in Bethsaida, talking and laughing and joking with all these people from the Davidson crowd.

She still hadn't seen me. Just as I was winding up my courage to go and speak to her, Tom greeted me.

'Ben! How are you, my friend? Did you have a nice day? We've had a great day.'

'That's good. Tom, were all of these people with you today? I mean at your meeting, on the mountain-side, or wherever it was?'

'Yes. All of these, and lots more besides. Is dinner ready? I'm famished.' And he wandered off to look for it.

The crowd had now drifted out of the porch and into the courtyard, where they stood around in little groups of three and four, still talking and laughing and joking, clearly in an excited and happy mood. I looked for Rachel, and spotted her talking to two other women under one of the palm trees. They were deep in conversation, smiling and talking nineteen to the dozen. I stood back in the shadow of the porch and watched them, feeling like an outsider at a family party—until Rachel looked up and saw me. Her face lit up, and she hurried across to me. In fact, she almost ran.

She threw her arms around me and hugged me. 'Oh, Ben. It's wonderful to see you again. It's wonderful to see you *here*.'

I returned her hug. Holding Rachel in my arms was magic. All the unease and disquiet of the day fell away from me. For several minutes we held each other in silence. Then she stepped back and looked at me. And Rachel smiled, that wonderful smile that came from her heart and shone through her eyes.

'Now that I've found you again, Rachel,' I said, swallowing hard, and finding it difficult to speak, 'I don't want to let you go again. Not ever.'

'Perhaps you don't have to,' she said quietly.

Then she took me by the hand and led me to a seat in a quiet corner of the courtyard. We sat down side by side, and Rachel took my right hand, a rather broad hand with stumpy fingers, in both of her small, soft hands.

'It's been a wonderful day for me, Ben, wonderful. I want to tell you about it.'

'And I want to hear about it, Rachel. Tell me.'

'I've seen him, Ben!'

'Seen who?'

'Jesus. Seen him. Heard him talk. And I can tell you it's true, Ben: he is alive!'

'Now, Rachel—'

'I know how you feel, Ben. At least, I think I do. But you're so close to the truth, if only you could see it.'

'I'm a rational man, Rachel, a reasonable man.'

'Am I unreasonable, then?'

She had me there. I always thought of her as having a more practical and down-to-earth intelligence than me.

'If it was just me, Ben, I wouldn't have believed it. I might have thought that I was seeing a vision, or a ghost, or. . .something, I don't know what. But it wasn't just me. This afternoon, on that hillside, there must have been, oh, five hundred of us, I guess.'

'I can imagine the scene. Peter, or maybe one of the others, was making a stirring speech, piling on the rhetoric, painting pictures with words, working you all up—until it got to the point where you all had a mass hallucination, and you all imagined that you were seeing the same impossible thing at the same time.'

'No, Ben, it wasn't like that at all. There were a lot of us, but it wasn't a rabble-rousing meeting. Nothing like that at all. We were sitting on the grass, talking in small groups, when, suddenly, Jesus was standing among us. Of course, we all felt the electric thrill of his presence. But that was after we saw him. Not before. It was not a "mass hallucination". It just wasn't that sort of thing at all.'

'And you said he talked to you? What did he say?'

'Well, he sort of unpacked the scriptures. He explained the real significance of things we have known all our lives. He quoted the law of Moses, and the Prophets, and the Psalms, and explained their meaning.'

'So, what is the meaning? What sort of conclusion did he come to?'

'Oh, I can quote his final words almost exactly, I

remember them so well. He said, "You are witnesses of these things. Therefore go into all the world and tell the good news to all people everywhere and make them my disciples and teach them to obey everything I have commanded you. And I will be with you always, to the end of the age". That's what he said.'

'Yes, but why, Rachel, why? Why should you, or anyone else, do that? What's the point?'

'Ben, you, of all people, should understand the point. In your work you've seen a lot of the seamier side of life, a lot of the cruel and awful things that people do to people. You only need to look at the headlines in the *Jerusalem Times* any day of the week to see that there is something wrong with this world. This is a broken world, Ben, and it needs mending.'

'And the mending of it is what this is all about?'

'That's exactly right!'

'Let's go for a walk, and talk somewhere a little quieter.'

Rachel took my hand, and we walked through the porch, and out onto the street.

'Just once around the block, Ben,' she said. 'Then I really should go and give them a hand in the kitchen. There are a lot of people to cook for tonight.'

As we started to walk slowly down the street, hand in hand, I couldn't help glancing at the other side of the street: the black car was still there.

'You were saying that the mending of this broken world is what it's all about?' I said, trying to put the black car out of my mind.

'Yes. This is a world in need of rescue. And that's what Jesus is about. He is God's rescue mission to humanity.'

'And his painful death, and return from the dead, are all part of that rescue mission?'

'Precisely.'

'There's an old maxim in the detective business, Rachel—it's all in the text books. "When you have eliminated the impossible, whatever remains, however improbable, must be the truth".'

'That sounds reasonable.'

'It is reasonable,' I said.

'But I don't see how it applies in this case,' she said.

'Don't you see that Jesus coming back from the dead has to be ruled out from the beginning? It has to be eliminated as one of the impossibles. Things like that just don't happen.'

For a minute or two Rachel was silent, then she said, 'Do you remember when we met in Jerusalem three days ago?'

'Yes, I remember. Vividly.'

'I asked you a question then. Let me ask you the same question again. Do you believe in God?'

'And I'll give you the same answer. Yes, of course I believe in God.'

'If you really believe in God, and if you believe that God is God—that he is the Greatest Conceivable Being—then your whole category of the "impossible" is eliminated. For as long as the world has existed God has done things like taking a tiny seed, causing it to fall into the ground and be covered over, virtually dead and buried. And out of that seed he has grown a giant tree, full of life, and growth, and fruit. That's the pattern of God's work, and you can see that pattern again in the resurrection of Jesus. God can't do the *logically* impossible, he can't, for example, make a square circle. But there is nothing that is *physically* impossible for him. If there was he wouldn't be God.'

This was getting pretty deep, and pretty difficult for me to follow. Rachel always was just a bit more intelligent, and a bit more widely read than me. At Jerusalem University I had done Law and just scraped through. She had done Philosophy and got lots of "A+" marks and won a university medal.

'So you see,' she said, 'the one thing you cannot say is: "Things like that don't happen". If God is God then it is a possibility. So, either you believe in God, and it is all possible, or you don't believe in God and then you have to explain away things like the empty tomb, and the amazing change in the disciples.'

'What change?'

'What change! Just three weeks ago they were defeated, dispirited, disheartened, scattered. Look at them now. They are more alive, more motivated, more inspired than any people I know!'

'Yes,' I admitted reluctantly, 'I guess that's true.'

By this time our talk had carried us all the way around the block, and we were back at the front door of the Boanerges house.

'The trouble is, Rachel, I am committed to rationality, to reason. All the pieces of the jigsaw haven't fallen into place for me yet.'

'They will, sweetheart, they will. I know they will. But right now I must dash and help the others in the kitchen.'

And with that she gave me a kiss on the cheek, squeezed my hand, and hurried inside. As I turned to follow her I couldn't help glancing over my shoulder at the other side of the street. The black car was still there.

Chapter 34

That night dinner was served in the courtyard. Long trestle tables were set up, and chairs and benches seemed to materialise from nowhere. It appeared that Zeb and Sal were used to feeding lots of people.

During dinner I sat with Rachel on one side and Tom on the other although, to be honest, Tom didn't get a lot of my attention. In between courses, Rachel and I reminisced and laughed at all the same old jokes again. The years apart fell away.

At the end of the meal old Zebedee stood up and pounded the table in front of him to attract attention.

'Silence! Silence!' he bellowed. 'Looking around me I see that there is a jolly sight too much washing up for the servants to handle. Therefore, speaking on behalf of every member of my gender present at these tables, I volunteer that the men shall do all the washing and wiping up.'

This was greeted by laughter and cheers from the women, and loud melodramatic groans from the men.

Thus it was that half an hour later I found myself

standing in the doorway of the kitchen with Tom (the kitchen was too full of other washers and wipers for us to fit inside) wiping up plates and cups and pots; the whole operation being run with military precision by old Zeb.

'How is your investigation going now, Ben?' asked Tom, as he handed a dried plate in through the doorway, and collected a wet one.

'I don't know exactly how to answer that. I've got more bits and pieces of information than you could shake a stick at. But it doesn't sort of fall together. At least, not into the nice, simple, commonsense shape that I'd like it to fall into. What on earth I'm going to report when I get back to Jerusalem, I have no idea.'

'In that case, Ben, old friend, there is someone I'd like you to meet. She might just be the key that locks everything into place for you. On the other hand, of course, she might not be.'

His last words prompted me to say, 'There's still a lot of the sceptic in you, Tom.'

'And it doesn't do me any harm at all,' he replied with a laugh.

'Anyway, who is this woman?'

'Her name is Mary Magdalene,' said Tom.

Mary Magdalene! That name that went back to the beginning of my investigation. It was first mentioned by the tart in the bar. Then I'd gone to the house in Jerusalem trying to find her, and Cleopas and Publius the soldier had both mentioned her as the first person at the tomb on that Sunday morning.

'Yes,' I said, 'that's someone I'd very much like to meet.'

After all the washing and wiping up was finished we went back into the courtyard, where only one of the trestle tables was still standing. It had been shifted back against one of the walls, and was loaded now with jugs of wine and rows of drinking goblets. All the carriage lights had been turned on, and the courtyard was flooded with a warm, yellow glow.

Tom took me by the arm and led the way through chatting groups of people, towards a group standing beside the well.

'Ah, here we are,' he said, and called, 'Mary!'

At that, five women turned around.

'Sorry,' said Tom, 'there really are too many of you.' He led me over to the group and introduced me.

'Mary, this is Ben Bartholomew, the chap I was telling you about. Ben, this is Mary Magdalene.'

The woman before me looked like one of those intelligent, strong-willed women that Katherine Hepburn used to play in the movies. In fact, she bore quite a strong resemblance to the young Katherine Hepburn.

'Delighted to meet you, Bartholomew,' she said, and shook my hand as vigorously as any man I ever met. 'What can I do for you?'

'I'd like you to tell me your story,' I said. 'Tell me exactly what happened in Jerusalem three weeks ago.'

'With pleasure. Get yourself a drink, Bartholomew. We'll find somewhere quiet to sit, and I'll be happy to tell you.'

A few minutes later we were seated on a cedar bench under a palm tree, and Mary Magdalene started her story.

'To begin with, you'd better understand that I won't describe what happened on the Friday. It was too painful, and the memory is too fresh, to talk about that yet. I will one day, but not yet.'

'Fair enough. Start on the Saturday night. What happened then?'

'Well, I guess I sort of took charge of matters. Rather a habit of mine. I had decided that it was our responsibility, us women that is, to see that the body of the Master was properly cared for. So, as soon as the sun set and the Sabbath was over Joanna and Salome and I went shopping and bought all the spices and oils that are needed to embalm the body properly. We couldn't have done it on the Friday—there hadn't been time.'

'But you knew where the body was?'

'I really don't want to think about that Friday, Bartholomew, but, yes, one of the other women and I (another Mary, in fact) had followed Arimathea and Nicodemus (at a distance) and we knew where the tomb was. It was arranged that, first thing on Sunday morning, I would lead the other women there to do the necessary embalming.'

'But you couldn't sleep that night?'

'That's right. You've heard some of this story before, haven't you, Bartholomew?'

'Some of it.'

'After the tension of that week, and the loss of the Master, I couldn't sleep. About an hour before dawn I found myself wide awake. I knew I wouldn't get back to sleep, so, although it was still pitch black outside, I decided to go down to the tomb alone.'

'Why?'

'Because I knew what would happen when I got to the tomb. I would cry. And I don't like to let other people see me crying. There is some grief that is very private. So, I got up and got dressed. Everyone else in the house was still asleep. I left a note telling the other women where I had gone, and leaving them directions so that they could find the tomb without me.'

'And then you went straight to the tomb?'

'Yes.'

'You had no difficulty finding it?'

'None. I may have been grieving, but I'm not a nincompoop. The garden appeared to be empty, and when I came to the tomb, the stone had been rolled away. The tomb was open. Well, I'm ashamed to say it, but when I saw it like that, I panicked. I ran back to the house. Ran all the way, as fast as I could. And when I got there I found the other women had gone. They had found my note, and followed me, taking the spices and oils and so on with them.'

'So, what did you do?'

'I woke up Peter and John. They were both still dead to the world and I had to shake them awake.'

'And you told them that the tomb was open?'

'I was still panicking, Bartholomew, I admit that frankly. What I said to them was: "They have stolen the Master out of the tomb, and I don't know where they have put him!". That woke them up in a hurry, I can tell you.'

'Who did you think had stolen the corpse?'

'The priests, of course! The temple authorities. What I thought was... Well, no, I wasn't really thinking at the time. ...what I *assumed* was that the temple bosses had stolen the body so that the tomb could never become a martyr's shrine.'

'So, that's what you told Peter and John?'

'Something like that.'

'And what did they do?'

'Grabbed some clothes and ran off towards the tomb. I shouted the directions at them, and they shot off like a pair of rabbits. John is smaller and quicker than Peter, and, as they disappeared around a corner Peter was struggling to keep up.'

216

'You didn't go with them?'

'I beg your pardon, I did! But there was no way I could have kept up. I was still out of breath after my run back from the tomb, and I was starting to get a stitch in my side. So I couldn't run. All I could do was walk. But I walked as quickly as I could.'

'And then?'

'Well, it appears that I missed the others coming back. I missed the rest of the women making their way back to the house, and I missed Peter and John. In those dim, dark, early morning streets, it's an easy thing to do. So, by the time I got back to the garden it was empty again, or appeared to be. I've been told since that there were two guards hiding there, but I didn't see them.'

'Who did you see? Or what did you see?'

'This time when I came to the open tomb I went inside. Tell me, Bartholomew, have you ever seen an angel?'

(There it was again! Why were people always asking me that question?)

'No,' I replied, 'I've never seen an angel.'

'I saw two that morning. Inside the tomb. Seated on the shelf where the body had been laid—one at the foot, one at the head. But I didn't realise they were angels; that has only struck me since. At the time, my eyes were filled with tears, and all I could see were two men, two strangers, dressed in white. They asked me why I was crying and I told them. Then I turned away and walked out of the tomb. And somewhere in the garden I stopped, and leaned against a tree, and just wept.'

As she spoke she appeared to be re-living the moment. Tears formed in her eyes. They were strong eyes, large brown eyes, and it was disconcerting to see tears in them. One of the tears escaped and ran down a cheek.

'When I turned around,' she continued, 'I saw someone standing there. Not that I could really see much through my tears by this time. Well, I thought it was the gardener, and he said to me, "Woman, why are you crying? Who is it you are looking for?" So, I said to this gardener, or this man I took to be the gardener, "If you took him away, sir, tell me where you have put him, and I will go and get him". And then he said to me...he said...my name... He said, "Mary!" ...in that voice of his...so full of compassion...and I knew then...that it was him...it was Jesus.'

So, I thought, that's who the guard had seen her talking to!

'And I turned towards him,' said Mary, 'and I said "Master!" and I stepped towards him, I wanted to put my arms around him. The one who was my Teacher, my Master, my Lord was not dead: he was back! But he said, "Do not touch me, because I have not yet returned to the Father. But go to my brothers and tell them that I am returning to him who is my Father and their Father, my God and their God". And then he was gone. I turned round and ran back to the house as breathless and excited as a schoolgirl, and I told everyone exactly what I had seen and heard.'

Chapter 35

Later that evening the servants brought coffee, and later still the guests started retiring to bed. Not all of the crowd were sleeping at the Boanerges house. Peter, and some of the others, it appeared, were going to sleep at his father's home, just a few streets away.

After I had finished talking to Mary Magdalene I sought out Rachel and told her about the conversation. And now, with the gathering breaking up, she said to me, 'Well, it's been a long day, Ben, and I'll have to go to bed before I fall asleep on my feet.'

'Do I get a goodnight kiss?'

'Do you think you deserve one?' she asked with a smile.

'Of course I do!'

'Then you shall have one,' she said.

I took Rachel by the arm and led her into a pool of shadow cast by one of the courtyard pillars that was as private a place as we were going to find in that crowded household. And there she kissed me, a long, warm, lingering kiss. Then she said goodnight, and went off to one of the large bedrooms that had been turned into a women's dormitory.

A little later I was standing in the now half empty courtyard drinking a second cup of coffee when Tom came up and threw an arm around me.

'Ben, my friend,' he said. 'How did your interview with Mary Magdalene go?'

'Very well,' I replied.

'Has it helped?'

'Perhaps it has.'

Tom took a step back and looked at me. 'You're not giving much away.'

'It'll all be in my final report,' I said.

'You've got something on your mind, haven't you?'

'I confess that the little grey cells are working overtime just at the moment.'

'Good! Good! That's what we sceptics always say: asking questions and giving thought is the way to find answers. Unexamined assumptions are like unexploded bombs—they need to be pulled apart to find out what makes them tick!'

I could think of no response to that, so I made none.

'Well, if I stand here much longer,' said Tom, 'I'll have to prop my eyelids open with matchsticks to stay awake. Goodnight, Ben.'

'Goodnight, Tom.'

A wave of weariness swept over me, and I realised that it was time that I too hit the sack. But before I did there was one task I had to perform. I went to the front door of the house, opened it part way, and looked across the street.

By the light of a street lamp I could see that the black car was still there, and behind the tinted windows I could dimly make out a figure sitting in the driver's seat. Perhaps, I thought, not the same man, but someone. Shagmar had, clearly, ordered a twenty-four hour watch. But why? What move was he planning? I still couldn't figure that out.

Fifteen minutes later when I was in bed and ready to fall asleep, I still hadn't figured it out. Perhaps, I thought as I lay there, wrestling with the problem will keep me awake. But it didn't. I was asleep in minutes, and I slept more peacefully, and more soundly, that night than I had slept for a week.

When I awoke the sun was up and the house was a hive of activity.

After I had washed and dressed I went downstairs to look for Rachel. I looked in the courtyard, in the kitchens, all over the place. I couldn't find her anywhere. I asked everyone but none of them knew where she was. Finally, someone said, 'Check in the scullery. She was working there earlier this morning.'

And it was the scullery maid who said, 'Rachel? The pretty, dark-haired one?'

'That's her.'

'Oh, she went out to get the milk a little while ago. She should be back soon. The dairy farm just up the hill, that's where she's gone. She shouldn't be long.'

When I heard that I stopped worrying and went and had some breakfast.

One of the trestle tables was back in the middle of the courtyard laden with bread, and cheese, bowls of olives, and fruit, and pots of coffee.

Tom joined me, and we ate a leisurely breakfast interspersed with small talk.

After breakfast I went back up to my bedroom where I could work in private: there were things I had to record in my notebook before I forgot them. An hour of note-making was quite enough, and I came back downstairs to find Rachel.

But she was still missing. No matter where I looked—no Rachel. I went back to the scullery maid.

'Have you seen Rachel since I was here last?' I asked.

'No,' said the maid, 'and it's most annoying. We're now very low in milk. I wish she'd hurry.'

'She should have been back by this?'

'Oh, she should have been back half an hour ago, at least. I can't imagine what's happened to her.'

Neither could I. And that's what worried me. Suddenly a thought occurred to me—an alarming thought. I ran to the front door and flung it open. The black car was still there. At least, I thought, Rachel has not been dragged into it and driven away. I went back to the scullery.

'Where is this dairy farm you were talking about?'

'You go to the top of this street, turn left, and follow the road for about half a mile, you can't miss it. The road winds around a bit, but as long as you stay on it you can't miss the farm.'

'Thanks,' I said, and hurried out of the scullery.

In the courtyard I found Tom and borrowed his trail bike.

'What's the problem?' he asked as he dug into his pocket for the keys.

'Rachel's missing.'

'Missing?'

'Yes. She went out before breakfast, and she hasn't come back yet. I'm worried.'

'What about? That she might have had an accident, or something?'

'Something like that.'

'Do you want me to come with you?'

'No. Just let me check out where she went. If I can't find her there, I'll come back and let you know.'

Tom showed me where he'd propped the bike, against the side wall of the house. I started the machine, and took off.

The wind whistling in my face as I rode cooled me down, and did something to calm the rising panic in my guts. Rachel was a sensible, level-headed person. Not a person to take risks or the sort of person who attracted accidents. What could have happened to her?

The road the scullery maid had directed me to curved in a kind of slow zigzag up a rolling hillside. On both sides of the road were rich, green pastures. Grazing cows looked up at me as I swept past, their large, soft eyes completely uninterested in the idiot on the motorbike.

The entrance to the farm was marked by a sign that advertised: FRESH MILK CREAM BUTTER.

I bumped in over a cattle grid, rode through the front yard, and stopped the bike next to a large dairy shed.

Inside the shed I found a young man and woman, both dressed in overalls, hosing out the milking area.

'Excuse me,' I called out.

'Yeah, what is it?' said the young man, turning off the powerful jet of water.

'I'm looking for a young woman.'

'Yeah, so am I,' he said, with a laugh.

'Her name is Rachel,' I said, ignoring his feeble joke. 'Late twenties, dark hair, brown eyes, good looking. She was supposed to come here this morning to collect the milk for the Boanergeses.'

'I don't recognise the description,' said the young man.

'I didn't see anyone like that this morning,' said the young woman in overalls, as she walked over to join us.

'Anyway,' she added, 'no one's come to collect the

Boanerges's milk this morning. So, if that's what she was supposed to be doing, she never got here.'

'You both certain?' I asked.

They nodded.

I left the shed, climbed back onto Tom's trail bike, and rode—very fast—back to the house.

In front of the Boanerges house I brought the bike to a halt and sat for a moment, with the engine ticking over, looking at the black car opposite. Shagmar's hitman was again in the driver's seat. The driver's window was wound half-way down, and he turned and looked directly at me. It appeared that he was no longer concerned about being recognised. Why? For a minute I toyed with the idea of walking across the road and confronting him. But not yet, I decided, after a moment's thought, not just yet.

I rode the bike around to the side of the house, parked it, and hurried inside.

In the courtyard Tom and old Zeb were waiting.

'Tom told me about Rachel going missing,' said Zebedee.

'While you were out,' said Tom, 'Zeb and I searched the house from top to bottom. She's definitely not anywhere here.'

'And we asked everyone in the place,' added Zeb. 'No one knows where she is, and she said nothing to anyone about going out this morning—except to get the milk.'

For a few moments I paced up and down the courtyard, rubbing my chin thoughtfully. 'In that case, there's only one thing that can have happened. And I'm the only one who can do anything about it. This is my game now.'

With that I sprinted up the stairs and into my room. There I dug down to the bottom of my travel bag and pulled out my trusty .38 snub-nosed revolver. I checked the gun over, loaded it, slipped it into my pocket, and ran back down the stairs. Tom and Zeb were still standing in the courtyard, looking puzzled.

'Can we do anything to help?' asked Tom.

'Nothing. If I'm right, the game is now being played on my territory, and I'll take care of it. Zeb, remember that black car I pointed out to you?'

'Yes,' said Zebedee.

'It's still there. The driver is an agent for the Syndicate. And, unless, I miss my guess, Rachel has been kidnapped.'

'Kidnapped!' said Tom. 'Shouldn't we tell the police?'

'The police can do nothing to help when it's the authorities, the powers that be, that have done the kidnapping. No, I'll have to take care of this myself.'

'Is she in any real danger?' asked Zeb.

'Probably not just at the moment. They've probably kidnapped her to put some sort of pressure on me. They don't know it yet, but they've made a big mistake.'

'Surely there's something I can do to help you, Ben,' said Tom.

'I appreciate the offer, Tom. But if it gets rough I can handle myself better alone.'

Tom and Zeb looked at each other.

'Don't take any unnecessary risks,' said Zebedee.

'Good luck,' said Tom as he shook my hand. 'You get Rachel back safely, and don't get yourself killed in the process.'

'I won't,' I promised.

Chapter 36

I left the house through a back door, and circled around the block, so as to come up on the car from behind. As I came around the corner, I paused. There it was—the same black Peugeot that had been there for two days. The driver was leaning back, his head lolling against the headrest. I understood how he felt: a stakeout can be a very boring job.

I moved slowly towards the car trying to keep myself in line with what I hoped would be at the back of its rear-view mirror's "blind spot".

Then I took the last ten feet in a run, flung open the driver's door, grabbed him by his coat collar, pulled him out of the car, and flung him heavily against the side of the vehicle. While he was still winded and dazed I reached for my gun. I pushed the short barrel of the revolver into his stomach and clicked off the safety catch.

'Where is she?'

Instinctively his hand reached towards his jacket where a shoulder holster bulged.

'Don't even think of it,' I said, pushing the barrel of my gun even harder into his guts.

His hand dropped back to his side.

With my left hand I fished out his gun—a Browning automatic—and dropped it into my pocket.

'Now that you've got no hardware, you'll start giving me answers,' I said. 'Where is she?'

'Lay off me, Bartholomew,' he growled. 'You touch me, and your sweetheart might just get hurt.'

'I'll take that risk, slime-ball. Now, where is she?'

'There's no need to get nasty, Bartholomew. She's quite safe.'

'She'd better be. Where is she?'

'I don't know, exactly.'

'If I have to ask the question again, buster, I'll start blowing your toes off with this toy in my hand. Where is she?'

'On the way to Jerusalem—'

'And what happens when she gets to Jerusalem?'

He was slow answering, so I dug him in the ribs again with my gun.

'*Argh*... She'll be locked up.'

'Where?'

'I don't know. He doesn't explain all his plans to me. I just do what I'm told.'

'When was she picked up?'

'First thing this morning. As soon as she came out of the house. We had a second car here—one of the Syndicate's big limos. Two of the boys dragged her into it, and took off for Jerusalem.'

'If she's been hurt in any way,' I growled, and pushed the gun deeper into his ribs.

'She's all right I tell ya! She's in the back of a fast car, bound and gagged, speeding towards Jerusalem.

Apart from tying her up, no one's done anything to her—'

'You'd better be right. If you're wrong—if you've done anything to harm her—I'll come after you so hard you'll wish you were a slave in the salt mines of Cyprus.'

'You're big with the threats, Bartholomew, but it's all wind. You know that if you take on me, you take on the whole Syndicate. And that's like taking on a herd of Carthaginian elephants single handed. You may be tough, Bartholomew, but you're not that tough.'

'Get into the car,' I said. 'Get in and drive. And remember, this gun is looking at you the whole time.'

Without taking the gun off the creep for one second, I climbed into the passenger's seat, and watched him while he climbed into the driver's seat.

'Start it up, and get moving,' I growled.

'Where are we going?'

I had to get rid of him fast but I hadn't made up my mind where, so I just said, 'Head for the lake.'

A mile or two down the lake road, I spotted a fisherman's hut on the shore, surrounded by trees and shrubs.

'Pull over here,' I snapped, got him out and into the deserted one-room hut—which stank of fish.

'Give me your belt, then put your hands behind your back.'

I switched the gun to my left hand, and with my right I made a loop out of the belt, slipped it around his wrists, and pulled it tight.

'Now, kneel down on the floor.'

He did it. Hanging on the wall of the shed was an old piece of electrical flex. I used it to tie his ankles together.

'Now, creep, talk fast. What were you supposed to do with me?'

By now he wasn't looking so tough. He was sweating and looking frightened.

'I was supposed to wait twenty-four hours then tell you that we had her.'

'And then what?'

'I was to tell you to go back to Jerusalem, and do exactly what Shagmar told you to do when you got there—if you ever wanted to see your girlfriend alive again.'

'And that's all you know?'

'That's all! I swear it!'

I believed him. He was too frightened to be lying. I pulled his handkerchief out of his top pocket, stuffed it into his mouth as a gag, walked out of the hut, and pulled the door closed behind me. I climbed behind the wheel of the black car, turned the keys, and kicked the engine into life. It was a six cylinder, twin overhead cam shaft, fuel injection, sports car, and the engine throbbed into life with a murderous roar.

This is the car I need, I thought, this will get me to Jerusalem long before I am expected, and that gives me a small advantage of surprise over the Syndicate.

Chapter 37

I drove back to the Boanerges house, and ran the black car into the driveway. Tom was at the front door ahead of me and as I went to knock he flung it open. 'Have you found Rachel?'

'No, not yet,' I said. 'But I was right—she's been kidnapped by the Syndicate.'

'Well, Bethsaida's not a big place—we can soon turn this town upside down, and find out where they're hiding her.'

'She's not being held here,' I explained, as I sprinted up the stairs to my bedroom with Tom beside me.

'She's on the way to Jerusalem in the back of a fast car.'

'Why? What do they want her for?'

'To put pressure on me. It's something to do with the case—an insurance policy to make sure I do whatever it is they want.'

As I spoke I hastily stuffed a few essentials into my small travel bag and Tom was scooting around the room picking up shirts and socks.

'If you're thinking of going after her. . .you'll never catch her. . .in a fast car, with a couple of hours start—'

'Well, I also have a fast car, you know. The Syndicate lent it to me'—Tom raised his eyebrows—'It wasn't their idea, of course. It was mine.'

'Oh. . .I see.'

'They'll still be in Jerusalem before me. But I'll be much closer behind them than they expect. And that will give me some advantage.'

I looked around the room to make sure that I had forgotten nothing, and ran back downstairs again, with Tom at my heels.

In the courtyard Zeb asked for news of Rachel and Tom brought him up to date.

'What are you planning to do, Ben?' asked Zeb, turning to me.

'Rescue Rachel, Zeb. Break her out of wherever she's being held—before they even realise I'm in Jerusalem.'

'Can you do it?'

'This is my kind of game. And Jerusalem is my patch. I can do it.'

'Is there anything I can do to help, Ben? Anything at all?' asked Tom.

'Actually, there might be. When are you returning to Jerusalem?'

'Probably tomorrow.'

'In that case, would you drive the Landrover back to Jerusalem for me? You see it's not my car—I borrowed it from a friend.'

'Just give me the address, and I'll return it.'

'Thanks, Tom,' I said. 'You're a real friend.'

I pulled one of my business cards out of my pocket, and wrote Sam Solomons' name and address on the back. Then Tom and I went out to the back of the house where the Landrover was parked. I made sure he understood how to drive it, grabbed a few things from the back . . . and then I remembered the beeper.

I detached it from under the mudguard and stood there with the little black box in my hand, wondering what to do with it. Just then, a sad-eyed, cud-chewing cow stuck her large head over the back fence and stared at me. Around the cow's neck was a bell on a leather strap. That, I thought, is the answer.

I walked slowly and cautiously towards the animal, so as not to frighten her. She stood calmly—obviously very tame and used to people—while I clipped the beeper onto the strap, next to the bell. If Shagmar had an agent monitoring the signal, it would appear that my vehicle (and I) were still safely in Bethsaida.

That last piece of deception accomplished, it was time to leave for Jerusalem. I threw my travel bag in the back of the Peugeot sports car, sat in the driver's seat, and turned the key in the ignition. The engine purred beautifully into life.

Tom reached in through the window and shook my hand. 'Take care of yourself,' he said. 'And Rachel.'

'I shall,' I promised him.

Then Zebedee came out of the house with a bag of fresh fruit and a water canister. 'You'll need something to keep you going and you won't want to stop.'

'Thanks, Zeb, that's kind of you,' I said, as I backed out onto the road. Then I turned the car, and hit the accelerator. With a roar like thunder, the car took off. In the rear-view mirror I could see Tom and Zeb waving farewell, and dwindling rapidly in size as I shot down the street with the power of six well-tuned cylinders.

In the town centre I turned right, and, within minutes, was well on my way.

The day was turning into one of those hot, still, humid days for which the Galilee valley was notorious. The car was the wrong colour for hot weather. On the other hand it had tinted windows and, I discovered, air conditioning, so my return journey to Jerusalem was going to be not only much quicker than the trip north, but more comfortable too.

The road around the lake was now leading me south-west, and it wasn't long before I had to slow down to pass through Capernaum. Then the road turned more directly south, through Gennesaret and Magdala in rapid succession. After that came a long stretch with no towns, and I brought the Peugeot up to something close to its top speed.

By the time I was roaring past the turn-off to Tiberias the air was as hot as the breath of the sphinx in the middle of summer. Just past Tiberias the road turned directly westward, towards the escarpment that fringed the valley.

On the way up the zigzag road that climbed the face of the escarpment I had to slow down a little—it's not safe to whip around the hair-pin bends too fast. I was struck powerfully by the sharp contrast between this return journey and my trip down the escarpment in the old Landrover, crawling slowly and cautiously through heavy rain and a thunderstorm.

Before long I was on the crest, and Lake Galilee was a thousand feet below. Up here on the plateau the air was pleasantly cooler, and I could turn off the air conditioning, and open the sun-roof.

By mid afternoon I had stopped at Nazareth for a tank of petrol, and turned left at the main T-intersection, onto the Great North Road that would carry me into Jerusalem. This time I would not take the long detour through Bethany, on the assumption that, by now, the Romans would have cleared the Zealots off the section of the road, just north of Jerusalem, that they had blocked.

As the sun set I was barrelling down the long, straight stretch of Roman highway leading to Sychar, pushing the sports car to its limit.

About nine o'clock at night I slowed down as I came into Sychar. On the right hand side of the city square, was 'The Wellview Motel' where I had stopped overnight on my journey north. This time I halted only to re-fill the tank with petrol, and to make a phone call to Shagmar in Jerusalem. I wanted to call him before I got into the Jerusalem city limits, the beeps would make the call sound like a long-distance one.

The phone was answered before it had rung twice.

'Hello.' The growling voice was unmistakably Shagmar's.

'If you have touched a hair on her head, I will kill you, Shagmar, with my own hands—slowly and painfully.'

'Oh, it's you, Bartholomew,' chuckled Shagmar. 'You weren't supposed to be told that we have your girlfriend until tomorrow morning.'

'Don't blame your agent too much, Shagmar—I made him talk.'

'You must care for this young woman even more than I imagined. Good, good.'

'Unless you're bullet-proof, Shagmar, don't touch—'

'Don't worry. She's quite safe—under lock and key, and no one will touch her. . .as long as you do exactly as you are told.'

'What is it you want from me?'

'Where are you calling from?' asked Shagmar, ignoring my question.

'Bethsaida,' I lied.

'In that case, get into that battered old vehicle of yours, and drive to Jerusalem at once. If you drive all night you will be here by morning. Do that. The sooner this business is resolved the better.'

'All right I'll do it. But what is required of me?'

'The Boss will be in his office tomorrow morning at eight o'clock—you be here to meet him. He will tell you then what you are required to do.'

'I've said I'll be there. In the meantime, you see that Rachel is—'

There was a click, and the line went dead. Shagmar had hung up.

Chapter 38

Back in the car I took a swig of water from the canteen, gulped down an apple, kicked the engine into life, flicked the lights onto high beam, and charged off down the highway, eating up the miles like a starving hyena devouring a carcass.

About midnight I passed the back road from Bethany that I had used on my journey north, thankful that I didn't have to use it again this time. Then I hit the stretch of road where, a few days earlier, the Zealots had ambushed a Roman regiment, but there were no road blocks up, and the highway appeared to be open.

Nevertheless, it was not the time to slow down. The Zealots were stubborn guerrilla fighters, not mere hit-and-run bandits. Within five minutes there was a sound like the world exploding, as a bullet smashed through the windscreen. After the first wild swerve I flicked off all the car's lights, and hit the accelerator so hard I almost pushed it through the floor. I didn't care who was doing the shooting—all I wanted to do was to get out of there.

There was another shot. Then two more...and I was through.

Fortunately the moon that had been bright enough to make me such a target also lit up the ribbon of road as it unrolled before me. I shot towards Jerusalem more like a low-flying aircraft than a sports car.

About an hour and a half later the road dipped down for a while, and then began to climb up the ridge to the city. It was two o'clock in the morning when, lights on again, I drove through the city gate and into Jerusalem.

Now I had to act quickly—in six hours time I had to be in Caiaphas' office, and by then I must have taken charge of the situation. The first priority was to rescue Rachel.

On the way down the Great North Road I had turned over in my mind the various places where they might be holding her, and it seemed to me there could be only one. Caiaphas, I decided, would want Shagmar to keep Rachel close to him and under his direct control. She couldn't be held in the temple itself but next door was Caiaphas' palace. And, according to underworld gossip, in the basement of the palace there were cells—dungeon cells. That was where he would have put Rachel. I was sure of it.

I drove towards my office, parked the Peugeot in Coppersmith Street and locked it, hurried down the alley, up the stairs, and let myself into the office with my pass key.

I unlocked my 'burglary' cupboard and pulled out the contents. First I changed into black woollen slacks, and a black jacket that I kept for exactly this purpose, and changed from my leather shoes to rubber-soled sneakers.

Then, from a bottom drawer, I pulled out the gladstone bag that contained a complete burglary kit made up of items taken from professional burglars encountered on stolen-property recovery cases. From the bag and into my pockets went a set of skeleton keys, a set of pick-locks, and a pencil-thin torch. A short, tempered-steel crowbar fitted into a specially made long, thin pocket inside my black jacket; a flat, metal flask filled with chloroform, and a pad of gauze, slipped into my back hip-pocket. I then strapped on my shoulder holster, and slipped my gun into place under my left armpit.

Now I was ready.

I locked the office and returned to the car. Slowly and quietly, with only the parking lights on, so as not to attract attention, I drove across town to the network of narrow streets and lanes that surround the temple. There, in the smallest, most out-of-the way alley I parked and locked the car, dropped the keys through a grating into a drain and continued on foot.

A few minutes later I was looking from the shelter of a dark doorway across to the palace of Caiaphas. Sweeping up towards the main doors was a broad stone staircase but what I wanted was a back entrance.

Keeping to the shadows I scouted the building. Sure enough, on the southern side was a low, iron door, set into the solid brick wall.

But between me and the door a patrolling guard appeared. As he turned the south-eastern corner of the building, I took out my watch. He was back in six and a half minutes, having done the circuit. That might be just enough time for what I had to do.

As soon as he was out of sight, I crossed the street,

into the shadow of the iron door and tried each of my skeleton keys—none of them worked. I glanced at my watch—five minutes. One more minute to struggle with the lock, half a minute to reach my sanctuary and the guard came around the corner of the building again. At least he was keeping to a steady pace.

Next time I tried the pick-locks, and the wards began to shift inside the lock. I had lifted several of the pins and partly turned the cam, when I glanced at my wrist watch—six minutes! I leaped into the shadow of a parked car just in time.

The guard came around the corner, strolled slowly down the length of the wall, rounded the corner at the far end, and I went back to the lock. A few more minutes of feverish work and the last of the pins fell into place, the lock clicked and I swung open the iron door. Inside, I found myself standing at the end of a narrow, dimly lit, stone corridor. I pulled the iron door closed behind me, and latched it into place. Now it was time to find Rachel.

I crept silently down the corridor, gently trying the handle of each door. The third one swung open slowly at my touch. I peered cautiously inside. A guard was sprawled across a small table, snoring loudly, a half-empty bottle of whisky beside him. If he was supposed to be patrolling the corridors of the building, I was in luck.

The next door along the corridor was solid wood, with a small, barred grill in its upper panel. On the other side a flight of narrow stone stairs led downwards. This would be the door I wanted. It was locked.

It was either waste time with skeleton keys and try to pick the lock or creep back to the drunken guard and risk waking him. I went back, relieved the still snoring guard of his keys and easily found a large, brass one that fitted the lock of the barred door. It swung gently back on its hinges and I crept down the stairs.

At their foot was a long, narrow, dimly lit corridor. At the end of it, I found a sharp turn to the left. With some apprehension I peered around the corner, and there, not six feet away, was another guard. This one was not in a drunken sleep, but very much awake and active.

For the moment he had his back to me, bending over a small table waiting for an electric kettle to boil. He appeared to be making himself a cup of coffee. Beyond him was a line of cell doors.

One of those cells—almost certainly—held Rachel!

Chapter 39

I reached into my back hip pocket for the bottle of chloroform and the pad of gauze. Next I soaked the pad in chloroform and returned the bottle to my pocket. With the chloroform pad held firmly in my right hand, I stalked forward, as stealthily as any jungle cat, until some shadow, or movement, or small noise gave my presence away and he started to turn. But it was too late. I leaped at him, clasped the chloroform pad firmly over his nose and mouth, and grabbed the back of his neck with my left hand to ensure that he could not escape the anaesthetic. He was a big, strong brute, but I had caught him unawares and got a firm grip before he could stop me. The more he kicked and struggled, the more deeply he breathed and the quicker the chloroform began to work.

After a minute or so he suddenly stopped struggling and fell limp in my arms. I held the chloroform in place until I was certain that he would be punching out the *ZZs* for a few hours then began my search of the cells.

The doors were solid timber in the lower half and barred in the upper half, all set in solid iron frames. Cell after cell was empty. Four of them. Five of them. Six of them. I began to despair.

Then, in the eighth cell someone—a woman—was lying on a bunk in the corner.

'Rachel?' I called softly. 'Rachel, is that you?'

The figure stirred. I flashed my penlight through the bars. I'd found her!

'Rachel!' I called, loudly this time.

She propped herself up on one elbow on the bunk. 'Who's there?'

In reply, I turned the penlight onto my face.

'Ben!' she cried out with alarm, 'Ben, they have caught you too?'

'Oh ye of little faith! I'm here to rescue you.'

And with that she leapt off the bed, ran over to the door, and reached her fingers through the bars to touch mine. There were tears in her eyes.

'Are you all right? They haven't hurt you?'

'No, Ben. I'm just very, very frightened, that's all.'

'Well, everything's going to be all right now. Just hang on while I get the keys from our friendly neighbourhood jailer, and I'll get you out of there.'

I ran back to where the guard lay on the floor, extracted a large keyring, and confronted the door to Rachel's cell. In the middle of it was a large, brass lock. By trial and error I found the right key. The lock turned with a satisfying clunk but the door refused to budge.

'There's a second lock,' said Rachel, 'somewhere near the top. I think it's a combination lock.'

I checked the top of the door frame. She was right. 'Oh great! And I've just put the jailer to sleep for a couple of hours.'

'But, Ben, I think only Shagmar knows the combination.'

'Then I'll just have to find some other way to open it.'

I extracted the crowbar from its pocket in my jacket and set to work to jemmy the lock open. My first six attempts were unsuccessful, but on the seventh the stone lintel that the lock slid into began to splinter. I realised then that the stone was the weakest part of the lock, and went to work on it feverishly. Bit by bit I chipped and splintered away fragments of stone until the bolt was held by only an eighth of an inch of rock. Then I dug the crowbar in deep, and pushed my whole weight against it. With a satisfying crunch the door sprang open, and a second later Rachel was in my arms, clinging to me and sobbing.

'Oh Ben! Oh Ben!' she sobbed.

'I love you, Rachel,' I heard myself saying.

But the celebration couldn't last for long.

'Come on. We've got to get out of here. First I'll have to take care of our chum at the end of the corridor.'

Rachel pressed herself back against the wall while I dragged the hefty guard along the narrow corridor and into the cell that she had just vacated. Once there I bound his hands and feet with sheets and stuffed a gag into his mouth. Then I swung the cell door closed and key-locked it. I didn't want Rachel's absence to be discovered too soon.

'All right, let's get out of here. Stay close behind me.'

And she did. I could feel the delightful warmth of her body very close behind me as we crept up the dungeon stairs, and out into the basement corridor. I locked the door at the head of the dungeon stairs behind us, and left all the keys with the still sleeping, drunken guard in the guardroom.

In this upper corridor Rachel and I were able to walk side by side, arms around each other. I glanced at her. The tears were gone, and her face looked strong and determined. Now that, I thought, is my kind of woman.

When we reached the iron door that would let us into the street I realised that we had a problem. The problem was the guard who passed the door every six and a half minutes.

'Wait here,' I whispered to Rachel.

I stepped up to the door, slipped back the latch, and eased it open a crack. Then I waited, with one eye on my watch. After three and a half minutes the guard passed on patrol. After he had gone I gave him a minute and a half to get around the corner of the building and well away. Then I swung the door wide open, and stepped out into the street. It was deserted.

'It's okay,' I said to Rachel, 'come on.'

She followed me out into the street. I set the latch back into the locking position, pulled the iron door to, and heard it lock behind us.

Then I took Rachel's hand in mine and we hurried across town.

'I need to get you to a safe house,' I explained, 'and I think my house is likely to be safer than yours— once they discover you are missing.'

'What about your parents? It's four o'clock in the morning.'

'They'll be delighted, don't worry about them.'

On the way through the deserted streets I explained why Rachel had to go to my house straightaway and why I couldn't stay with her.

'I have to be in Caiaphas' office at eight o'clock,

and I have a job that I have to get finished before then.'

'Is that safe? Going to see Caiaphas, I mean?'

'I think so. And if everything works out as I intend, it will make our lives a great deal safer.'

At my house I let us in through the front door with my latch key. We tip-toed into the lounge room, turned on the light, and turned to each other.

'I haven't thanked you yet,' whispered Rachel, 'for rescuing me.' She stepped forward and threw her arms around me. 'Thank you, darling,' she said. 'Thank you.'

And then she kissed me. And I kissed her. And that went on for quite some time.

Eventually I said, 'When we're married, I suggest we go to live in Caesarea, or somewhere like that, on the coast at least. Not that Jerusalem will necessarily be all that unsafe, it's just that somewhere else is bound to be safer.'

'Hold on,' said Rachel. 'Did I hear something about "married" in there?'

'Um...well...yes, you did.'

'That was a proposal was it?'

'Yes, I guess it was.'

'Well, you might give a girl a chance to respond, mightn't you?'

'You want a chance to respond?'

'Yes please.'

'Okay, then. Rachel, sweetheart, will you marry me?'

'Yes, I'd love to.'

And then we started to kiss again but we were interrupted by a cry of delight from the doorway.

'That's wonderful! Just wonderful! Rachel! Benjamin!' said Mama. 'My heart is melting with pride and happiness. I'm so pleased for the both of you.'

Then Mama hugged Rachel and Rachel kissed Mama on the cheek, and then I hugged Mama and Mama cried on my shoulder, and then Mama went upstairs to wake up Papa and tell him the news. I kept saying I had to go but it was five o'clock in the morning before I got away to put the second half of my plan into operation.

'Now, Rachel,' I said as I was leaving, 'if I'm not back here by nine o'clock, something has gone wrong, and you must go straight to Sam Solomons' place—they won't think to look there. Sam will hide you for a few days, at least until Tom turns up with the Landrover. When he does you go with Tom—your friends will protect you.'

'What about you?'

'If I don't come back this morning, it will be too late to worry about me. Don't come looking for me.'

'Do you have to go?'

'If I don't the danger is greater.'

Rachel hugged me, with tears in her eyes. 'You take care of yourself.'

'I will. I promise you, I will.'

With that I dragged myself out of her arms, and jogged across town to my office. Fifteen minutes later I was sitting at my desk with the Davidson file and my pocket notebook spread out in front of me. For the next hour and a half I worked on bringing the case notes up to date, with every fact recorded, and a complete set of conclusions deduced from them. Then I bundled the case notes into a manila envelope and hurried across town to the home of a lawyer. I caught the man I wanted while he was having his breakfast, and over his bowl of Crunchy Flakes I explained what

I had in mind. He thought it was a great idea, and was delighted to take the file off my hands.

By then it was almost eight o'clock, and time to meet Caiaphas—for the final confrontation.

Chapter 40

At exactly 8 am I knocked at the same small back door to the temple court that I had been taken through on the first day of this case. It felt as though a year had passed since then, but it had only been a week. When the door was opened by a guard, I stepped inside, pushing the door wide open as I did so.

'Tell Shagmar, Bartholomew is here,' I said.

As it happened Shagmar was in the corridor just behind the door. He looked up, startled, when he heard my voice.

'Surprised to see me, Shagmar?'

'My electronic surveillance unit told me you were still in Bethsaida!'

'Put not your faith in electrons, my son. Now, take me to Caiaphas.'

Still looking a little stunned, Shagmar led the way. Two minutes later I was in the same long, dark, heavily curtained room in which Caiaphas had given me the assignment a week before.

'Mr Bartholomew to see you, Excellency,' growled

Shagmar, and took up a position near the door—presumably to prevent my hasty departure.

'Ah, Mr Bartholomew, how kind of you to call,' whispered Caiaphas in his soft, sibilant, threatening voice.

'My pleasure,' I lied. 'You want me to do something for you—what is it?'

'You're a very direct man, Mr Bartholomew, very direct. I like that. And I will tell you exactly what I require, and precisely what you are going to do.'

He paused for a moment to pull his dark robes more closely around his shrunken body, and then continued.

'You are a man of some celebrity, Mr Bartholomew. Your recovery of missing persons, especially of runaway teenagers, has attracted considerable media attention. There have been feature articles about you in newspapers and magazines. You have been interviewed on radio and television. You have that precious commodity—credibility.'

'You're making me blush, Caiaphas—so what?'

'Mr Shagmar's agents have kept a close watch on your investigations, and we know that you have been unable to produce the body of Jesus the Nazarene. That being the case we switch to Plan B. The reason we hired you, Mr Bartholomew, was precisely because of your celebrity, and your credibility. Plan B involves using that credibility. We want you to write a report for us, Mr Bartholomew, an official report of your investigation. You will say in that report exactly what we tell you to say. We will issue copies of your report to the press. You will make yourself available for interviews. You will very convincingly argue that every word of your report is true.'

'And what, exactly, do you expect me to say in this report?'

'You will say that you succeeded in proving that the disciples stole the body of Jesus Davidson. You will further say that you tracked the body to Galilee—where they had taken it.'

'And then the press will ask me to produce the body. What do I say then?'

'We've thought of that, Mr Bartholomew. You will say that you personally observed these disciples take the dead body out onto Lake Galilee in a boat, put the body in a sack weighted with stone, and sink it in the deepest part of the lake. No one will ever be able to prove that you are not telling the absolute truth.'

I had to hand it to old Joe Caiaphas—it was a cunning plan.

'And what if I refuse?'

'As I am sure you already know, Mr Shagmar is holding under close detention a young woman who is, I am told, quite dear to you. Her physical well being, indeed her very life, depends upon your co-operation, Mr Bartholomew.'

'Think again, Caiaphas...Rachel is no longer in your cells.'

'Shagmar, is this true?' snapped Caiaphas.

Shagmar strode forward, grabbed a phone on the desk, and punched up a number. 'Check the cells at once!' he rumbled into the phone in his voice of gravel.

For the next two minutes the three of us sat in the kind of icy silence that any passing penguin would have recognised as resembling an arctic midnight in midwinter.

Presumably Caiaphas and Shagmar were considering what their options were if I was correct. I knew—and they didn't—that I still had one more card to play.

The phone buzzed, and Shagmar grabbed it.

'She's gone,' he reported to Caiaphas, as he hung up the phone. For a moment the Syndicate boss and his muscle-man looked at each other, then Caiaphas nodded.

Shagmar walked over to where I stood, folded his giant hand into a huge fist and punched me in the chest. As soon as I saw the blow coming I stepped back. But I was too late. The blow caught me hard, and knocked me across the room. I struggled to my feet, winded and sore and trying to catch my breath. I braced myself for a second blow, but it never came.

Shagmar, it appeared, had suffered more than I had. From the agony on his face, and the way he was holding his hand, I would guess that he had broken one, or possibly two, of his fingers.

Then I remembered I was still wearing my burglary outfit. Shagmar's fist had collected the crowbar that sat in its special pocket in my jacket.

'Get down to the infirmary,' snapped Caiaphas, 'and get that seen to. I will take care of our impertinent young friend here.'

Shagmar slunk out of the room.

Caiaphas was now holding a small, silver-plated revolver in his hand.

'Sit down, Mr Bartholomew,' he said. 'You and I have things to discuss. You will still do just what we want you to do. We have ways of making you obedient.'

'I'm quite sure that you have a hundred nasty things that you could do, if you wanted to. But are you sure that it would be in your best interests to do so?'

'What do you mean?'

'Before coming here this morning I wrote up my case notes on the Davidson affair. Those case notes are now complete. And I have placed them for safekeeping into the hands of a lawyer. You may have heard of him—his name is Nicodemus ben Gorion. He is a powerful man, a member of the Sanhedrin, and a member of one of the noble families. You dare not touch him. He will keep several copies of my case notes in high security in several different places. So, even if you have one of your hired thieves break into his office safe, you can never be certain you have obtained all the copies. And if anything happens to me or to Rachel—if we die, or disappear—Nicodemus will send those case notes to the press. Not just to the *Jerusalem Times* but to every newspaper from Rome to Cairo.'

'And what, exactly, do these case notes of yours contain?'

'All the facts. Everything, from the day you brought me here and briefed me—all the information and testimony I gathered, the interviews with the eye-witnesses, the interview in my office with Lord Annas (Yes, you know about that, don't you?), the evidence I gathered in Galilee—everything.'

'I see. . . I see.'

'In addition the report contains the conclusions I have deduced from the evidence.'

'So tell me—what deductions did you make?'

Chapter 41

In the first place I deduced that there are six—and only six—ways that the body could have been removed from the grave. One: Jesus could have revived and walked out. Two: thieves could have stolen the body. Three: the Romans could have taken it. Four: you, the temple authorities, could have taken it; or—five: the disciples could have taken it. We'll leave number six to one side for the moment.

In my report I consider each of those possibilities.

Number one is out. Jesus was dead. I checked up on that. People just don't survive crucifixions, and Roman executioners don't make that kind of mistake. Crucifixion is a common occurrence, and Roman soldiers are experts at it, having reduced it to an exact science with a set of rules to be followed. As I say— they know their job well (and with good reason). And it was more than their lives were worth to make a mistake when dealing with Jesus, since the governor, Pilate, had personally condemned him to death.

Even if this bizarre theory were true and Jesus only

fainted and revived, in his weakened condition there is no way he could have escaped from the tomb. But, in the end, what really knocks the socks off this one is that Jesus could not, and did not, survive his crucifixion.

As for number two—the theory that grave-robbers stole the body—you, Caiaphas, know that didn't happen. I'm sure I'm not the only line of investigation you've pursued. You would have had Shagmar's agents looking everywhere. If ordinary thieves had taken the body you would have recovered it, and put it on public display, by now.

Besides, the only items of value in that tomb were the linen shroud and the jars of spices left by Nicodemus and Arimathea—but they were *left untouched* when the body disappeared! No thieves would do that. So, the body was not taken by thieves.

Since your henchmen told the guards to lie about the disappearance of the body, why didn't you bribe some common thieves to say they had stolen it? The answer to that is: you knew they would never have been believed. Too many people in Jerusalem know the condition of the empty tomb for such a story to hold water. But the bottom line is: if thieves had stolen the body, you would have recovered it and displayed it by now. You haven't, so they didn't.

Third: just in order to cover all bases, I considered the possibility of the Romans' taking the body. The trouble is that they would have absolutely no motive for doing so. All that Pilate wants is to stay out of local political and religious disputes. You yourself know how hard it was to get him to sign the death warrant. All he wants to do is wash his hands of the matter, and have no further trouble. I repeat—there was no conceivable motive for the Romans to take the body.

Anyway, why would they provide a guard, and then steal the body they were guarding? Pilate has already run into hot water over bringing the Roman standards into the city, and over raiding the temple funds for public works. The very last thing Pilate would ever countenance would be any action that cast another shadow on the quality of his administration. Clearly, the Romans didn't take the body.

Fourth: it occurred to me that you might be playing some double game, and might have taken it yourself. On the Sunday morning the body vanished, the first woman at the tomb—Mary Magdalene—thought that your priests or guards must have stolen the body. But if you had the body you would have produced it to stop this rumour of resurrection.

You could have destroyed the credibility of the disciples, and caused all their claims to be dissolved in a gale of laughter—simply by producing the body. There is nothing you would like to do more. Therefore, you don't have the body, and that's another possibility eliminated.

Fifth: did the disciples take it? I've met them. I've interviewed them. And the answer is: "No". As Nicodemus pointed out to me, the psychology of it is all wrong. You and Lord Annas both admitted to me that the crucifixion succeeded in dispersing and disheartening and all but destroying the group. On the third day after the violent death of their master, there is no way they could have re-grouped, re-organised, and stolen the body.

And anyway, if the disciples did this, why have they not been charged with stealing the body? According to Roman law the body of a condemned criminal belongs to the state. That's why Joseph Arimathea had to ask Pilate's permission to bury Jesus. To steal a body is a serious offence and it is certainly strange that neither you, nor the Roman authorities, have preferred charges against the disciples, or done anything to substantiate the story you told the guards to spread. By the way, in court I could destroy the story those guards were ordered to tell with a single question—in cross-examination I would say to them: 'If you were asleep, how do you know what happened?' And that lying story your henchmen fed the guards would be laughed out of court.

No, the fact is, the disciples were depressed, afraid and leaderless. There is no way they could have taken the body. That's a possibility that just won't hold water.

So, then, what did happen?

Well, all the evidence can be classified under two categories: the Empty Tomb, and the Appearances.

As far as the tomb is concerned I have collected sufficient statements from witnesses to have a clear understanding of who came and went, and when, at the garden tomb on that Sunday morning. You'll find all the details in my report. (If you like, I'll have Nicodemus send you a copy.) And it is clear that there was no human agent who had the opportunity to steal the body. But *the fact of the empty tomb remains*—it is the one hard, unavoidable fact that must somehow be explained.

It is the one fact that everyone agrees on—all the disciples, the Roman guards, even you, friend Caiaphas, admit that the tomb was, and is, empty. Remember, the disciples didn't expect it. On that Sunday morning those women went to pay their last respects at what they believed was their Master's last resting place. It was to their absolute consternation that they found, not a body, but an empty tomb.

Even then, the other disciples had to be persuaded that the tomb was empty. On top of which, the first reaction of Mary Magdalene, the first disciple at the tomb, was that the body must have been removed by the authorities. The disciples were not expecting an empty tomb, and were just as bowled over by it as anyone else. The empty tomb is the rock-hard, central fact that any solution to the puzzle must explain.

As for the appearances, you can read for yourself the eyewitness accounts of these. They do not bear the marks of hallucinations, or visions, or dreams. They sound as matter-of-fact as eyewitness reports of a road accident. They are clearly reports of what people have personally experienced.

Hallucinations occur when someone longs for something so much that eventually they believe it has happened. So for hallucinations to have happened the disciples must have *expected* Jesus to rise from the dead. But the reverse is the case. Mary Magdalene did not see a gardener near the tomb and imagine it was Jesus—she saw Jesus and imagined he was the gardener! The two disciples going to Emmaus did not see a stranger and think he was Jesus—they saw Jesus and thought he was a stranger.

The truth is that it was not the disciples who convinced themselves that Jesus was alive—it was Jesus who had to convince them. And he succeeded in convincing down-to-earth fishermen like Peter, John and Jim, and hardened sceptics like Tom.

And, anyway, hallucinations are highly individualistic and subjective—they don't happen to whole groups of people (up to five hundred at a time)! The only rational account for the appearances is that Jesus really appeared.

From this evidence there is only one logical

conclusion to be drawn (this is the sixth possibility that I left off my list earlier): God took the body out of the tomb. God is certainly capable of doing it, after all God is God. We have an old saying in the detective business: when you have eliminated the impossible, whatever remains, however improbable, must be the truth.

Everything else has been eliminated. Hence, we must accept the improbable truth—that God brought Jesus back to life, and brought him out of that tomb.

If you, friend Caiaphas, lift a finger against Rachel or me, that is the report that will be splashed all over the media: that Jesus is back! That he is in business again, recruiting and inspiring disciples. And that death—the final enemy of humanity—has been conquered for all who will answer his call and acknowledge his kingship in their lives.

Two days later Rachel and I were sitting on the bus to Caesarea, all our possessions in three suitcases in the bus's luggage rack. With my parents' blessing, and because of the continuing need for safety, we had gone to Bethany to wait for the other disciples at the home of Martha and Mary. Rachel had explained that the disciples always stopped there on their way to Jerusalem.

And it was there that Peter had married us, and the local rabbi had registered the marriage. Now we were heading for Caesarea, and a new life—together.

'Tell me again what you said to Caiaphas,' said Rachel.

I told her again.

'I wish I could have been there to see his face. You

were very clever, dear, bringing the case to such a successful conclusion.'

'Well, it's nice to think that my last case was a successful one.'

'Your last case? What's this all about?'

'Well, I think the private detective game is no business for a married man. So when we get to Caesarea, well out of the reach of the authorities in Jerusalem, I thought I'd dust off my old law degree and hang out my shingle as a local lawyer. I thought a quiet life might be a good idea.'

'Sounds delightfully dull, my sweet,' said Rachel.

'So the Case of the Vanishing Corpse is the end of my career as a detective.'

'But this is not an ending, darling, it's a beginning,' said Rachel, 'the start of a whole new adventure, not only for us, but for the rest of the world as well.'

And you know, I've got a feeling that she was right.

Calling all Armchair Detectives

Would you like to conduct your own investigation into Ben Bartholomew's Case of the Vanishing Corpse? Well, you can.

You can become an 'armchair detective'. Copies of the original eyewitness reports are readily available (in the New Testament part of the Bible) for you to scrutinize, along with other books of evidence, analysis and argument.

Here are some quick guidelines for all would-be armchair detectives.

As any good historical detective will tell you, what matters is going back to the original source documents. You'll find these, as I have mentioned, in the New Testament. There are four historians who record the firsthand eyewitness accounts, their names are Matthew, Mark, Luke and John. I recommend reading them in a clear, reliable modern translation. The one called *The Good News Bible* is first class.

Continuing your armchair detection, what other evidence, analysis and discussion is available?

Well, if you wish to investigate the reliability of the historical data, the book I recommend is called *Is the New Testament History?* by Paul Barnett. (Another book by the same author, called *Bethlehem to Patmos*, is the best available summary of the history of the New Testament period.)

There are other steps you can take. There is no shortage of evidence and data for you to investigate. For a start, you might want to re-read this book, and go back over the evidence that Ben Bartholomew found so convincing; and there are two other books I would like to recommend. To introduce them, I must explain that if you decide, as an armchair detective, to investigate the Case of the Vanishing Corpse, you will not be the first person to do so.

In the late 1870s two men were sharing a railway carriage, travelling across the mid-west of the United States. As they journeyed they fell into an argument over whether the resurrection of Jesus was historical fact, or mere fiction. One of them argued vehemently that the story was pure fiction, an absolute fraud. After arguing for some considerable time, this man made a wager: he would carefully research all the historical facts, and then he would put his research into a book proving that Jesus did *not* rise from the dead.

In the months that followed he did his research diligently and thoroughly, and that research changed his mind. In the end, the book he wrote took the opposite line to the one he had originally expected—he wrote a book to demonstrate the *truth* of the resurrection.

The man's name was Lew Wallace, and the book he wrote was a novel called *Ben-Hur*—subtitled, *A Tale of the Christ*. The book became a best-seller, it was turned into a spectacular stage play, and has twice been made into a movie—each one being a huge box-office success and winning numerous awards. *Ben-Hur* was first published in 1880, and is still in print today.

Lew Wallace was an active soldier for much of his adult life, serving with distinction in the Mexican War and the Civil War, and rising to the rank of major-general. Wallace also served as governor of New Mexico and as American ambassador to Turkey. He was not a man who could be fooled by weak or shoddy evidence. And he became absolutely persuaded that the resurrection of Christ was not fiction or fraud, but solid historical fact.

A similar story is told by Frank Morrison in his book *Who Moved the Stone?*, first published in 1930, also still in print. The first chapter of that book is called 'The Book that Refused to be Written'. In it Morrison writes: 'When, as a very young man, I first began seriously to study the life of Christ, I did so with a very definite feeling that, if I may so put it, his history rested upon very insecure foundations'.

He goes on to explain that he planned to research and write about the subject in a book he intended to call *Jesus, the Last Phase*. His intention in this book was to tell the story, and to 'strip it of its overgrowth of primitive beliefs and dogmatic supposition'. He then explains what happened.

I need not stay to describe here how, fully ten years later, the opportunity came to study the life of Christ as I had long wanted to study it, to investigate the origins of its literature, to sift some of the evidence at first hand, and to form my own judgement on the problem which it presents. I will only say that it affected a revolution in my thought.

In the rest of the book Morrison shows how the

historical evidence persuaded him that a story he had previously thought impossible was, in fact, the plain truth. *Who Moved the Stone?* is not a novel, but a vivid and highly readable book of history.

There are many others who could tell the same story as Lew Wallace and Frank Morrison. Over the past two thousand years there must be millions who, as 'armchair detectives', have pursued the same investigation, and discovered the same truth. I know— I am one of them. Which leads me to the question, gentle reader: What about you?

So, go to it armchair detectives—lay your hands on a copy of the eyewitness reports in the New Testament and let your investigation begin.

And remember, your investigation really matters. In *The Case of the Vanishing Corpse* I have one of the characters explain that: 'If all this is untrue then it doesn't matter. But if it is true it matters enormously. The one thing it cannot be is true and unimportant'.

CLUES FOR ARMCHAIR DETECTIVES:

a study booklet to accompany
The Case of The Vanishing Corpse

by Kel Richards

ISBN: 1 875245 13 8

for use by study groups, scripture classes, youth fellowships is available from:
St Matthias Press PO Box 225 Kingsford NSW 2032 and Christian bookshops.